Misdeeds and Mistletoe

This Christmas, the ornaments aren't the only things breaking

Tumblebrook Christmas Mystery

Ellen Le Teace

Bradford Press

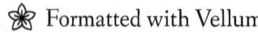

Chapter 1

Winter Lights at the Inn

T he first snow of December had been polite about it.

It had drifted in overnight while Tumblebrook slept, sugaring the gabled roofs and lining the sidewalks in soft white. By morning, the town looked like the front of one of the Christmas cards displayed on the mantel in the Tumblebrook Inn's lobby—pine boughs dusted, lampposts capped, the frozen surface of Tumblebrook Lake blushing pale pink beneath a rising sun.

Inside the inn, it smelled like cinnamon and oranges and just the tiniest hint of wood polish, because Amelia Farnsworth refused to let even Christmas be an excuse for smudged banisters.

She stood at the foot of the main staircase with a spool of red velvet ribbon in one hand and a pair of scissors in the other, surveying her domain.

The Tumblebrook Inn sparkled.

Garlands twined up the banister, woven through with fairy lights and tucked with sprigs of evergreen and baby pinecones. Wreaths hung on the interior doors, each slightly different—a nod to her guests' penchant for "authenticity" that she'd learned from the tourism blogs—one with juniper and blue berries, another all cinnamon sticks and dried orange slices.

In the lobby, the big stone fireplace was already lit, flames snapping softly beneath a mantel crowded with framed photographs, candelabras, and an army of vintage nutcrackers that had once belonged to her grandmother. The couches wore their winter slipcovers—plaid wool in deep red and forest green—and every side table boasted a small bowl of peppermint bark or gingerbread cookies shaped like cats.

And in the center of it all, towering from floor to ceiling, stood the Christmas tree.

"Perfect," Amelia murmured, though she knew better than to say it too loudly.

The tree had been a production. Clara had stood in the snowbank in front of the inn, gloved hands planted on her hips, shaking her head at the ones they'd rejected.

"Too sparse," she'd said of one. "Too crooked. Too...enthusiastic," of another with branches that seemed to stab outward at aggressive intervals.

But this one, now resting in the corner where guests liked to take pictures, was just right. Grand, but not ostentatious. A full sweep of blue-green boughs, strong branches, the faintest whisper of pine in the air whenever someone passed by. Its ornaments—carefully arranged after three separate attempts—were a curated blend of vintage glass baubles from her grandmother's collection, wooden snowflakes carved by Ezra from up on the hill, and an assortment of more modern pieces: ceramic mugs, knit hearts, a miniature sleigh.

Lady Grey, of course, hated it.

The grey British Shorthair sat beneath the tree now like a plush gargoyle, amber eyes narrowed, following Amelia's descent with grave suspicion.

"Don't even think about it," Amelia warned, because she knew that look. That calculating, whisker-twitching look.

Lady Grey blinked, slow and regal, then stretched one paw up as if casually, casually, she might test the swing of the lower ornaments.

"Don't you dare," Amelia said.

Lady Grey's paw rose higher. Her claws flexed.

Somewhere in the kitchen, a timer dinged—a high, insistent sound that meant Clara needed a hand. Amelia gave the cat her firmest innkeeper stare.

"I am watching you," she said, and dashed toward the kitchen.

By the time she barreled through the swinging door, she could hear the faint, crystalline *tink* of glass hitting glass.

"Lady Grey!" she called over her shoulder.

Clara Henderson looked up from the sheet pan she was sliding from the oven. Her cheeks were flushed from the heat, her curls pulled back into a messy knot that had somehow attracted a dusting of flour.

"Was that you or the cat?" Clara asked.

Amelia blew out a breath and leaned against the counter, inhaling a wave of sugar and butter and cinnamon. On the island, a battalion of gingerbread men smiled up at her, flanked by stars and trees and a few vaguely cat-shaped blobs.

"The tree," Amelia said. "She's at it again."

"Lady Grey has artistic differences with your ornament placement," Clara said dryly. "Honestly, she might be right. The red ones are a little bottom heavy."

"I thought guests would want them in their photos," Amelia said. "And I've already done the whole thing three times. If I have to unknot one more strand of lights, I'm going to start charging them extra for 'atmosphere.'"

Clara chuckled and set the pan on a cooling rack. Outside the kitchen window, Amelia could see the world just beginning to wake. Doris Finch's café sign flickered on down the street. The lampposts along Main Street still glowed, their wreaths catching the early light. A couple of bundled-up locals trudged past, one balancing a cardboard carrier from Misty Lake Coffee Co.

This was Tumblebrook at its best: snow-dusted, festive, humming with the promise of the Winter Lights Festival.

"How many batches does this make?" Amelia asked, nodding at the cookies.

Clara glanced at the recipe card, smudged at the edges with cocoa powder. "Seven. We still need at least three more if we're going to survive the onslaught. You know what happens when the children's choir finishes their set."

"They descend like adorable locusts," Amelia said.

"Exactly. But at least they smile while they destroy us."

The Winter Lights Festival was Tumblebrook's pride. For one long weekend, the sleepy North Shore town became a destination. Tourist buses arrived with people clutching thermoses and cameras. The downtown businesses competed in a window-decorating contest. There were carriage rides and carolers, a Christmas market, and the crowning glory: the Lights Walk down by the lake, where the trees were wrapped in shimmering strands that reflected off the ice like stars.

This year, for the first time, the Tumblebrook Inn was the official festival headquarters.

Which meant they were full.

Which meant, as Amelia's grandmother would have said with a twinkle in her eye, there was no room for nonsense.

Unfortunately, nonsense had a way of booking under false names and sneaking in at the last minute.

"Speaking of nonsense," Clara said, as if reading her mind. "What's the latest on Mr. British Antique?"

"Edward Covington," Amelia corrected automatically. "He's not British. He just has strong opinions about tea."

"That's the same thing," Clara said. "Is he still arriving on the afternoon shuttle?"

"Yes. And please, for the love of all that is merry, don't call him Mr. British Antique to his face. He's kind of a big deal."

"He's an appraiser," Clara said. "He looks at shiny things and says, 'Yes, this is shiny, and also old.'"

"That shiny, old ornament he authenticated last year?" Amelia said. "It sold at auction for more than this entire inn is worth. The festival committee is over the moon that he agreed to judge the 'Heritage Ornament Showcase.'"

Clara shrugged and started transferring cookies to a cooling tray. "I just hope he doesn't mind cats."

Amelia opened her mouth to reply. From the lobby came another faint clink, followed by the unmistakable jingle of a displaced ornament rolling across hardwood.

She shut her eyes briefly. "I should go rescue what's left of my heirlooms."

"Tell Lady Grey she can't detective the crime scene until there's an actual crime," Clara said.

"Don't jinx it," Amelia said, grabbing a dish towel and heading back out.

The inn's lobby was a picture of holiday serenity—if one ignored the small grey cat perched halfway up the tree like an ornament with delusions of grandeur.

"Lady Grey!"

The cat froze, one paw wrapped around a branch, her back feet scrabbling for purchase between two strands of lights. A glittering red bauble swung precariously beneath her.

"Get down this instant," Amelia scolded, crossing the room as quickly as she dared without alarming the feline acrobat further.

Lady Grey, being Lady Grey, chose that moment to leap.

She landed with a thud on the arm of the nearest armchair, the red ornament batting wildly against the branch before plummeting toward the floor. In a move that would have impressed the town's hockey team, Amelia dove forward and caught it in the dish towel inches before it shattered.

She lay there for a second, half on the floor, half draped over the armchair, heart hammering as the ornament spun gently in the cradle of terrycloth.

Lady Grey hopped down and sat beside her, flicking her tail, clearly pleased with her human's reflexes.

"That," Amelia panted, "was a limited edition German glass ornament from 1949."

Lady Grey blinked. Her whiskers twitched.

"Yes, it was too low," Amelia said, hauling herself upright. "But some of us respect history, you know."

The front door opened with a gust of cold air and cheerful bell jingle, letting in a swoosh of snow and the sound of voices. Dora Jansen from the festival committee bustled in, arms full of clipboards and a rolled-up banner. Beside her, two volunteers wrangled a crate of fairy lights.

"Amelia! Isn't it just perfect out there?" Dora called. "The snow is cooperating for once. It's like someone ordered it in from a catalog."

She stopped short when she saw Amelia holding the ornament like a fragile heart.

"Oh, don't mind us," Amelia said. "I'm just saving family history from feline sabotage."

Dora clucked sympathetically. "Lady Grey has good taste. She only goes after the prettiest ones. That's a compliment, really."

Lady Grey, as if aware she was being discussed, hopped onto the registration table and sat on the stack of festival brochures, looking smug.

Amelia set the rescued ornament on the mantel for safekeeping, then helped Dora unroll the banner: WELCOME TO TUMBLE-BROOK WINTER LIGHTS FESTIVAL.

"Is everything still set for tonight?" Amelia asked. "Check-in table? Raffle baskets?"

"Yes, yes," Dora said, ticking things off on one of her clipboards. "The children's choir is rehearsing, the high school jazz band has promised not to play anything 'too modern,' and Doris is making enough hot chocolate to float the town. We just need you to be your charming self and keep our VIP guests happy."

"No pressure," Amelia murmured.

"You've done splendidly so far," Dora said briskly. "The rooms look darling. I peeked in the 'Sugarplum Suite' on my way past. The candy cane pillows! Inspired."

Amelia smiled, though her stomach did a small, anxious flip. Being the centerpiece of the festival brought attention, and attention brought expectations. She wanted the inn to be at its sparkling best— for the town, for her grandmother's memory, and, privately, for herself. After the year they'd had, a smooth, festive weekend sounded like the best possible gift.

Dora checked her watch. "The shuttle from Duluth should be here by three. That's our out-of-towners, including Mr. Covington. Do we have his welcome basket ready?"

"In the office," Amelia said. "Local jam, Misty Lake coffee beans, a brochure about the ornament showcase, and a sternly worded note reminding him that my grandmother's collection is for display, not for sale."

Dora laughed. "He does have a reputation."

"What kind of reputation?" Amelia asked lightly, but the question lingered.

"Oh, you know." Dora fluttered a hand. "Passionate about his work. Says what he thinks. There was some...minor kerfuffle about a misattributed Victorian bauble a few years back, but it only made him more famous. Controversy sells in his business."

Amelia thought of her grandmother's ornaments, each one with a story. Some had tiny slips of paper tucked into their boxes, handwritten notes about where they'd come from. Tucking them away after Christmas had always felt like tucking away pieces of her family's history—safe and waiting for next year.

She didn't love the idea of a man who courted "controversy" anywhere near them.

"He'll be on his best behavior here," Dora said, as if sensing her concern. "Besides, he's not just here for your ornaments. The festival committee arranged for him to judge the heritage showcase. He's a guest, not a vulture."

Amelia nodded, unconvinced but determined. "Then we'll make sure he has a very pleasant stay."

By midafternoon, the inn thrummed with additional life. Suitcases rolled over the threshold, bringing with them the sounds of zippers and the smell of foreign laundry detergent and expensive cologne. Guests shook snow from their hats, stamped their boots on the mat, and looked around with pleased surprise.

"It's like stepping into a snow globe," one woman murmured to her husband.

Amelia checked people in at the front desk, the routine movements soothing. Room keys, signatures, a quick explanation of breakfast times and the festival schedule. She recognized a few locals who'd booked rooms for the novelty of "vacationing" in their own town. Others were strangers, their cheeks pink from the cold, eyes bright with holiday excitement.

And then he arrived.

"Edward Covington?" she asked, though she already knew.

He was taller than she expected, with a kind of lean, practiced elegance that made his winter coat hang just so. His hair was more silver than the photos she'd seen online, combed back from a high forehead. He wore a charcoal scarf, black leather gloves, and the expression of a man who had seen one too many poorly decorated hotel lobbies.

When his gaze swept across the inn's interior and then returned to her, his eyes had softened a fraction.

"Ms. Farnsworth," he said, voice warm with a hint of something— Old Money boarding school? Theater training?—lingering in the vowels. "You've made a jewel box out of this place."

"Thank you," Amelia said, smiling. "Welcome to the Tumblebrook Inn. Long trip?"

"Long enough," he said, removing his gloves. His hands were

slender, ink-stained, the fingernails neatly trimmed. "But your snow is far more civilized than what I left behind in Boston. That was a blizzard. This is a postcard."

"We like to coordinate with local photographers," Amelia said lightly. "If you'll just sign here and here, I'll get you your room key."

He leaned over the register, his handwriting looping elegantly across the page. Lady Grey materialized as if from nowhere, jumping onto the desk and sitting squarely on the corner of the sign-in sheet.

"Ah," Covington said, pausing his pen. "Is this the famous Lady Grey I've heard about?"

"You've heard about her?" Amelia asked.

Dora, lurking nearby with a clipboard (of course), stepped forward. "We may have mentioned her in the festival brochure."

"We wanted our VIP guests to understand that they were entering a working inn," she added, "and that our Resident Cat would be freely roaming the premises, bestowing judgments and fur as she sees fit."

Lady Grey blinked at Covington, then head-butted his hand, leaving a faint trace of fur on his cuff.

"Charmed," he said dryly. But his eyes crinkled at the corners as he scratched under her chin. "I find cats to be excellent judges of character. Don't you, Ms. Farnsworth?"

"Generally," Amelia said. "Though she has been known to take bribes in the form of tuna."

"Don't we all," he murmured.

She handed him his key. "You're in the North Star Suite. Top of the stairs, second door on the left. We've placed a few of our simpler vintage ornaments in your room, as you requested, but the main collection is in the parlor showcase. I'll be happy to show you whenever you like."

He looked pleased. "I appreciate your trust."

"Mmm," Amelia said. "Trust, or close supervision. Take your pick."

He laughed—a short, genuine sound. For a moment, he was just a weary traveler charmed by a small-town inn. Then his gaze slid past her to the tree, and something sharpened in it, like a jeweler's loupe focusing on a flaw.

"That," he said softly, "is extraordinary."

She turned to follow his gaze. The tree glowed in the dimming afternoon light, its ornaments catching fire from the fairy lights. The silver sleighs. The blown-glass globes. The delicate bells.

Covington took a step closer, breath catching. "That snowflake—may I?"

"With supervision," Amelia said, moving with him and Lady Grey, who trotted along as chaperone.

Covington reached toward a glass snowflake near the middle of the tree, fingers hovering a respectful inch away, as if afraid his breath alone might crack it. "Hand-cut," he murmured. "1930s, perhaps. Not factory-made—see the asymmetry in the arms? There's a touch of the maker in it. And that bell beside it—good heavens, is that cloisonné?"

Amelia felt some of her tension drain. At least when it came to the ornaments, his reverence seemed real.

"They were my grandmother's," she said. "She collected them over decades. Not all of them are valuable, but they all have stories."

Covington's face softened. "The stories are the valuable part."

Behind them, the front door banged as more guests arrived, shaking snow from their shoulders. The inn filled with the rustle of coats, the murmur of conversation, the distant clatter of Clara slipping on a stray bit of flour in the kitchen and swearing under her breath.

"Tonight," Dora called, raising her voice so everyone could hear, "we'll be hosting a welcome reception right here in the parlor! Hot cocoa, cookies, and—if you behave—Amelia's famous mulled cider. Mr. Covington has graciously agreed to say a few words about our heritage ornament showcase."

Applause followed. Covington inclined his head modestly.

Amelia's stomach did that flip again, but this time there was a thread of excitement woven through. This was what she'd wanted when she'd decided to keep the inn going: moments like this, where strangers and neighbors mingled in front of a fire and the place felt less like a business and more like a living, breathing heart of the town.

But even as the inn glowed with holiday charm, a quiet unease threaded through the day, waiting for night to give it shape.

Chapter 2

Shadows in the Parlor

That night, when the sky had turned dark and the snow had begun again in fine, glittering needles, the parlor glowed.

Amelia had lit every candle she owned. The fireplace roared cheerfully, sending shadows dancing along the stone. The tree seemed to have grown more luminous, the glass ornaments catching the light like captured stars.

Guests crowded the room, balancing mugs of cocoa or cider and small plates laden with Clara's cookies. Someone started a low carol in the corner; others joined in softly, an impromptu choir.

Lady Grey made the rounds like a furry politician, weaving between legs, accepting gentle pets, occasionally sniffing at a plate of cheese as if to assess quality control.

Amelia stood near the fireplace, watching Covington from the corner of her eye as he circulated. He had a knack for focusing on one person at a time, making them feel as though their particular ornament or family heirloom story was the most fascinating thing he'd ever heard.

"And you say your grandfather brought it from Norway?" he asked an older woman who held a tiny glass bird cupped in her palm.

"Remarkable. See the detailing on the wings? That's distinctive to a certain workshop—"

He glanced up and caught Amelia's gaze across the room. For a moment, his face was open—pleased, almost boyish—and she smiled back.

Then the lights flickered.

It was just a small blink at first, like a wink. A murmur rose, then fell as they steadied.

"It's the wind on the lines," someone said.

"This old building and its wiring," someone else chuckled.

Amelia felt a prickle at the back of her neck. She made a mental note to call the electrician again, just as the lights went completely out.

The room plunged into darkness.

For a heartbeat, there was silence—thick, stunned. Then the jumble of voices rose: startled cries, nervous laughter, the clink of a dropped mug hitting the hearthstone.

"Everyone stay calm," Amelia called, relieved that her voice came out more or less steady. "The fireplace is still lit. We have candles. It's probably just the wind. Dora, can you—?"

"I'm right here," Dora's voice answered, a few feet away. "I'll check the breaker."

Lady Grey brushed against Amelia's calf, fur electrified, tail puffed like a bottlebrush.

"Stay close, sweetheart," Amelia murmured, bending to press a hand to the cat's back.

The lights flickered again, stuttering on for a moment at half-power, turning the room into a nightmare version of itself—shadows too long, faces pale and strange—then off again.

Someone in the corner laughed nervously. "Best haunted house I've ever been to."

The tree loomed, a darker shadow against the gloom, its string lights dead. The ornaments that had sparkled minutes ago were now just shapes, still and unknowable.

Amelia could hear her own heartbeat in the dark. The air smelled like wax and cider and a faint, metallic edge she couldn't place.

"Just a moment!" Dora called from the hall. "I think—"

The lights came back on with a pop.

Warmth flooded the room. The fairy lights on the garlands flickered to life. The lamps glowed. The tree reasserted itself as a thing of beauty, not menace.

For a moment, everyone laughed, relief bubbling up like shaken champagne.

And then the laughter dissolved into a shriek.

The sound came from near the tree—a high, keening note that sliced through the chatter and pinned everyone in place.

Amelia's gaze snapped toward it.

Edward Covington lay on the floor at the base of the tree.

He was on his back, one arm stretched toward the branches as if he'd reached for something. His eyes stared sightlessly at the ceiling, glasses slightly askew. His mouth was parted in what might, if Amelia hadn't known better, have been surprise.

In his right hand, he clutched a shattered ornament.

Red glass glittered on the hardwood around him like spilled rubies. The central piece of the bauble remained in his grip, jagged edges biting into his palm, a thin smear of blood marking where they'd cut him. Even from where she stood, Amelia could see that it had once been one of the rich, deep crimson spheres she'd hung with such care.

The room, which had been full of warmth and music and the clink of mugs moments before, was suddenly very quiet.

"Mr. Covington?" Amelia's voice sounded strange to her own ears—too high, too far away.

She moved forward, the crowd parting for her. Lady Grey trotted at her side, silent now, tail low.

Covington didn't move.

Amelia knelt beside him, the world narrowing to his face, his hand, the glittering shards on the floor. Somewhere behind her,

14

someone started to cry. Dora was saying something about ambulances, about the storm and the roads and the sheriff.

Amelia reached for Covington's wrist, feeling for a pulse she already knew she wouldn't find.

Nothing.

She swallowed hard against the rising tide of disbelief, of helplessness.

On the jagged curve of the ornament clutched in his hand, a faint smudge of gold lettering caught the light. She squinted, trying to make out the words.

For those who—

A chill skated down her spine.

She didn't need to read the rest to understand what Lady Grey already seemed to know as the cat sat beside her, eyes unblinking, focused on the still form beneath the tree.

The Winter Lights Festival had just become a crime scene.

Chapter 3

Clues and Cookies

Snow muffled sound in a way that felt almost holy. Even through the canvas walls of the bake-off tent, Clara could hear the hush roll over Tumblebrook like a heavy quilt—followed by the sharp, unmistakable sound of someone screaming from the direction of the inn.

Her first thought was of Amelia.

Her second, irrationally, was of the cookies in the oven.

"Keep an eye on those," she told a wide-eyed volunteer. "If they burn, so help me, I'll haunt this tent."

She bolted into the cold.

The wind hit like a wall, laced with stinging flakes that found every gap in her coat. Across the street, the Tumblebrook Inn blazed with light. People clustered in the doorway, silhouettes framed against falling snow. The bake-off's cheerful chatter had vanished, replaced by a charged stillness that made her heart pound harder with every crunch of her boots.

This was supposed to be a weekend of cocoa and carols, not screaming.

Clara pushed through the knot of onlookers at the door. "Excuse me—sorry—moving disaster triage coming through—"

Inside, warmth hit her in a dizzying wave—cinnamon, cider, evergreen... and panic. The cozy Christmas glow she'd left less than an hour ago had twisted into something sharper. The tree still sparkled. The fire still burned. But the center of the room had been carved into a clear circle of horror.

"Amelia?" Clara's voice rose above the babble.

Her friend turned, pale under the soft light, kneeling beside a man on the floor. Antique ornament fragments glittered around them like bloodied jewels. Lady Grey sat sentry-still nearby, golden eyes solemn and unblinking.

Clara's stomach dropped. "Oh no."

"Edward Covington," Amelia whispered. "He's gone."

The words seemed to flatten the air. A few guests gasped. Others instinctively stepped back, as if death might spread by proximity.

Clara crouched beside her, careful not to touch anything. Covington's expression was oddly peaceful now, the intensity he'd carried earlier erased. Only the broken glass in his hand betrayed violence.

"What happened?" she asked quietly.

"The lights went out," Amelia said, her voice distant, mechanical with shock. "Just for a few seconds. When they came back... he was like this."

Clara glanced around. Every face looked wrong in the flicker of firelight—too pale, too frightened, too honest or not honest enough. The tree loomed overhead, its ornaments suddenly less like decoration and more like witnesses.

"All right," she said, drawing a steadying breath. The practical part of her brain clicked into place with a soft, familiar thud. "We have to calm everyone down. We can't panic until we know what's what."

"That's easy for you to say," muttered Alden Pike from near the hearth. The developer from Duluth—broad-shouldered, slicked-back hair, gold tie clip catching every stray light—looked less haunted than annoyed. "We're trapped here. The storm's cut the road clean off. And you're telling me there's a body under the Christmas tree?"

"Mr. Pike, please," Clara said, slipping into her bookshop-clerk tone—the one she used when small children argued over the last sparkly bookmark. "Let's get people seated, maybe in the dining room. We need a headcount and some quiet while Amelia calls Sheriff Daniels."

A murmur rippled through the room. Some guests obeyed without thinking; others bristled, still trying to make sense of the unreality.

Amelia rose slowly, smoothing trembling hands down her skirt. "Sheriff Daniels," she echoed, as if hauling the thought up from the bottom of a deep well. "Yes. Of course."

Clara guided her toward the phone behind the counter. Snow lashed the windows, the wind a low moan against the glass, a reminder that the world outside had shrunk to inn-sized dimensions.

The call took less than a minute. Amelia hung up, eyes distant.

"The line's patchy, but I got through to the dispatcher," she said. "Daniels is snowed in up in Bear Creek. The plows won't clear the ridge until morning."

"So we're on our own," Clara said.

Amelia nodded. "He told us to stay put. Don't move anything. Keep everyone safe. He'll come as soon as he can."

Clara rubbed her chilled hands together, forcing herself to think. She'd spent years shelving mysteries at Gossamer Fables, arguing over red herrings with Mr. Lark, rolling her eyes at books that leaned too hard on coincidence. Fiction never quite prepared you for how loud real people sounded when they were frightened.

"Okay," she said briskly. "We can work with that. I'll get everyone together in the dining room. We'll make cocoa, light candles, keep them occupied. You... sit for a second, breathe. Then we'll go over what happened."

Amelia managed a faint, shaky smile. "Clara Henderson, crisis manager."

"Only until Daniels digs himself out," Clara said. "Then I'm going back to cookies."

She herded the guests gently into the adjoining room. The chatter buzzed—half fear, half gossip. Doris Finch clutched a napkin like a handkerchief, muttering that she knew this festival would bring bad luck. Mr. Lark, the bookseller, whispered to Ezra, the hermit artist from up on the hill, who looked as though he'd wandered into a dream he disliked and was hoping someone would shelve him elsewhere.

Alden Pike lingered by the parlor door, arms folded, impatience radiating off him like heat from the fire. Not frightened, Clara noted. Irritated. As if a man's death were an inconvenient scheduling conflict, not a tragedy.

She crossed to him. "Mr. Pike, I'll need everyone in the same room until the sheriff arrives. It'll be easier to keep track of who's where and make sure everyone's all right."

"I'm not some suspect," he snapped.

"No one said you were," Clara replied calmly. "The snow's bad, the phones are unreliable, and people are scared. I'd appreciate your cooperation just so we don't lose anyone in a snowdrift or a pantry."

He hesitated, jaw flexing, then sighed and stalked toward the dining room, muttering under his breath about small towns and small minds.

When the last guest was seated, Clara paused in the doorway and glanced back into the parlor. Amelia was kneeling again beside Covington's body, Lady Grey perched beside her like a soft grey cloud. The firelight made the shards of red glass gleam faintly, like tiny captured warnings.

The practical part of Clara's mind—always louder than the senti-mental—took over. Evidence. Clues. Order in chaos. If Daniels couldn't reach them until morning, someone had to start paying attention now.

She rejoined Amelia as Amelia rose from the body, face tight.

"Are you okay?" Clara asked softly.

"No," Amelia said honestly. "But I'm here."

"Good enough for now," Clara murmured.

She knelt carefully, taking pains not to disturb the broken ornament. On the edge of Covington's vest pocket, something white protruded—a folded tag or scrap of paper. She glanced toward the dining room to be sure no one was watching, then eased it free with two fingers.

A small gift tag, the kind tied to presents with ribbon. The handwriting was elegant, deliberate. Familiar in that general way all careful script resembled her grandmother's Christmas labels.

For those who lie to the stars.

A shiver crept up her spine. She remembered Amelia mentioning the smear of gold lettering on the ornament he'd clutched. For those who—

Similar phrasing. The same hand? A set? A message?

She slipped the tag into her apron pocket, feeling the cardboard press against her hip like a question.

Behind her, Amelia said softly, "What do you make of it?"

Clara jumped. "You shouldn't sneak up on people when they're trying not to contaminate evidence."

"I think that ship sailed the moment twenty people trampled the rug," Amelia said tiredly. "Anything?"

"Maybe," Clara hedged. "I'll tell you when I'm sure it's not just my 'I've read too many Agatha Christies' brain. For now, everyone's corralled in the dining room. I promised cocoa and cookies. If we don't follow through, there might be a second crime scene."

Amelia's mouth twitched. "Trust you to run a murder scene like a bake sale."

"People are calmer when they're fed," Clara said. "It's in the Bible somewhere. Or at least in a cookbook."

Together they moved to the kitchen. The familiar clatter of mugs and spoons steadied Clara's nerves. The cookies she'd abandoned, just delivered through the kitchen door were miraculously unburnt, the volunteer clearly taking her haunting threat to heart.

She set water to heat while Amelia dug out the cocoa tins with hands that still shook around the edges. The air filled again with cinnamon and chocolate—a fragile peace layered over fear.

"Who do you think could've done it?" Amelia asked after a long silence, voice low.

Clara watched the kettle, steam beginning to curl from the spout. "Too early to say. But someone here knows more than they're admitting. That's just math. One dead man, one room of witnesses, several secrets per capita."

"Mr. Pike, perhaps?" Amelia said slowly. "He certainly isn't acting like a man traumatized by what he just saw."

"He's more irritated than scared," Clara agreed. "And irritation takes confidence. He's hiding something, I'd bet my best gingerbread on it. Whether it's murder... who knows?"

"Doris argued with Covington, too," Amelia added. "About the Finch teapot at the charity auction. Dora mentioned a 'kerfuffle' last year over an ornament he misattributed."

"So we've got professional controversy, personal grudges, and one very dead appraiser," Clara said. "Festive."

They carried steaming mugs into the dining room. Conversation dipped as they entered, then resumed in hushed tones. The small comfort of warm hands around ceramic did its quiet work; shoulders loosened, breathing slowed.

"Everything's going to be fine," Amelia said, moving among them with practiced hostess calm that almost fooled Clara. "We'll stay cozy and safe until the sheriff gets through in the morning."

Doris Finch dabbed her eyes with her napkin. "He was right there, talking to me not an hour ago," she said shakily. "I told him his appraisal notes had the wrong dates. He said I didn't understand art."

"You argued with him?" Clara asked gently, offering a plate of cookies.

"Oh, nothing serious," Doris said quickly, as if suddenly hearing how it sounded. "A misunderstanding over the charity auction. I just wanted to be sure he'd listed the Finch teapot properly. It was my grandmother's." Her voice trembled. "Now he's—oh, it's dreadful."

Clara noted the detail—and the way Doris's gaze skittered away. Panic made tongues wag; wagging tongues revealed things.

Mr. Lark sipped cocoa with a thoughtful air. "I heard him mention a catalog earlier," he mused. "Said he was missing a few pages."

"A catalog of what?" Amelia asked.

"Antique ornaments, I suppose," Mr. Lark said. "He seemed quite intent on it. Said something about 'lost entries' and people pretending things were what they weren't."

Ezra shifted uneasily in his chair. "He asked me about my carvings too. Wanted to know if any of the nativity pieces came from old growth near the North Shore. He seemed... agitated. Like he was searching for something specific and not finding it."

Clara glanced at Amelia. The same thought passed between them: the ornaments. The inscriptions. The way Covington's gaze had sharpened when he first saw the tree.

A gust of wind rattled the windowpanes, making a few guests flinch. The storm had strengthened, the world outside reduced to swirling white. It would be a long night before help arrived.

Lady Grey wandered in, jumped gracefully onto the empty chair beside Doris, and curled into a dignified loaf. The simple, ordinary motion eased the room more effectively than any speech. A few guests reached out to stroke her; their voices softened, conversations settling into an uneasy but less frantic hum.

Clara slipped out, drawn back to the parlor.

The fire had burned low, embers glowing a deep, steady red. She found herself studying the scene again, tracing and retracing the story in her head like a familiar plot whose ending she couldn't quite recall.

Lights flicker. Panic. Darkness. In those seconds, anyone could have crossed the room. A shove, a poisoned drink, a hidden medical condition—it was all possible. And until Daniels arrived, it all stayed hypothetical.

She crouched again, eyes scanning for detail. A faint scuff on the floor near Covington's shoe. Wax dripped down one of the candles on the mantel, as if someone had bumped it hard enough to tilt. The broken ornament pieces formed a half-moon around his hand, as though he'd been clutching it when he fell instead of dropping it.

She tried to picture the moment: a man reaching for something—or someone—before collapsing. Glass shattering in his grip. The words on the tag in her pocket prickling at her like a burr.

For those who lie to the stars.

What did that even mean? A poetic flourish? A warning? A private joke only Covington and someone else understood?

Lady Grey padded in, tail high, and hopped onto the settee. She sat there, eyes trained not on the body but on the tree.

"Don't suppose you saw who did it," Clara murmured.

The cat blinked once, slow and knowing.

"Didn't think so. Worth asking."

A sudden crash from upstairs made her heart jolt.

Amelia appeared in the doorway, alarm flashing across her face. "What was that?"

"I don't know," Clara said, already moving toward the staircase. "Stay here—no, come with me. If I fall through a floorboard, someone needs to tell my story."

They climbed quickly, the creak of each step swallowed by the wind outside. At the top landing, a draft knifed through the hall—one of the doors ahead hung open, the brass number gleaming faintly in the dim light.

North Star Suite.

Edward Covington's room.

The lock had been forced, splintered wood jutting from the frame like broken bone.

Clara exchanged a grim look with Amelia. Her pulse spiked—not from the climb this time, but from the sudden, undeniable fact settling over them like fresh snow.

"Someone," she said softly, "just broke into a dead man's room."

And whoever it was wasn't waiting for Sheriff Daniels to start looking for something.

Chapter 4

Whiskers in the Dark

L ady Grey was not a large cat, nor was she one to flaunt unnecessary drama—unless, of course, the drama involved strings, ribbons, or anything fragile and expensive dangling temptingly at head height. But on this night, with the wind rattling the windows of the Tumblebrook Inn and the humans running around in a state of mild hysteria, she carried herself with grave purpose.

There was something wrong in her inn.

Lady Grey knew the place as well as she knew the rustle of her food bag or the sound of Amelia's footsteps at dawn. Every corner, every scent, every sunny windowsill belonged to her, woven into the quiet kingdom she managed with dignified precision. But what hugged the walls tonight—fear, tension, the sour tang of human worry—did not belong.

She sat at the top of the staircase, tail wrapped neatly around her paws, studying the closed doors along the hallway. The floorboards hummed faintly beneath her, carrying vibrations from the voices downstairs. Humans never realized how sound travelled through wood and plaster. Even whispered conversations reached Lady Grey if she cared to listen.

Tonight, she cared very much.

A murder. That's what the humans were calling it, in hushed tones that flickered like candlelight struggling against a draft. A man lying still beneath the Christmas tree. A shattered ornament in his lifeless hand. Too many booted feet stomping through her peaceful domain.

She did not like this at all.

Lady Grey's whiskers twitched as she lifted her head. A scent drifted down the hallway—odd, sharp, out of place. Peppermint. Not the pleasant kind Clara folded into cookies, but a cold, biting peppermint, the kind someone in too-formal gloves might keep tucked into a coat pocket. Always the same. Always a little too much.

Lady Grey disliked peppermint.

She rose, stepping soundlessly onto the carpet runner. The old blue pattern—chosen by her grandmother-human decades ago—was familiar, a map her paws had memorized long ago. She padded past the guest rooms until she reached the one left slightly ajar.

The North Star Suite.

Edward Covington's room.

Her ears flicked at the memory of the earlier crash. Strange noises did not frighten Lady Grey—they intrigued her. And something had happened here. Something important. Something her humans would not understand unless she guided them.

She slipped inside.

The door creaked softly. Humans believed cats made no noise at all—they were wrong. Lady Grey made noise only when she wished to be noticed.

The North Star Suite was dim, lit only by the faint spill of light from the hallway. Covington's suitcase lay open on the bed, its contents rumpled from someone's frantic search. Papers littered the desk. A drawer hung askew, one edge splintered as though it had been forced.

Lady Grey sniffed the air. Paper. Leather. Lavender cleaner. Cedar from the wardrobe. And that peppermint again—sharper here, fresher, clinging to the room like a warning.

Her tail lashed once.

Her pupils widened, pulling in what little light the room offered. Shadows sharpened. Corners deepened. She trotted toward the bed, leapt up, and examined the suitcase. Socks. A leather-bound notebook. Shirts folded with the fussiness of a human who ironed even their thoughts. Nestled among them were loose sheets—one torn at the edge, as though ripped quickly from a binding.

Covington had been reading.

Or the intruder had been searching.

Lady Grey sniffed the pages. Peppermint. Paper. Ink with a faint, bitter tang.

She hopped down and padded to the desk. With a practiced spring, she jumped onto the chair and then onto the writing surface. A row of pencils rolled beneath her paw. She tested them—mostly for fun. Humans believed neat rows meant order. Inefficient, but charming.

Then she saw it.

A glint under the rug near the desk leg. Something pale and thin, one corner curled.

Lady Grey moved toward it, lowering her nose. This paper was different—older, dustier, with the faint glue-and-ink scent she recognized from Covington's clothes. She'd smelled it earlier on the ornament he'd clutched.

Whatever this was, it mattered.

She hooked one claw under the rug and tugged. Rugs were heavy, stubborn things—blankets foolishly nailed to the floor—but she had patience and purpose.

The scrap came free.

She sat upright, tail curled elegantly, examining it. The paper held part of an illustration—an ornate curve that might have belonged to a lantern or the corner of a decorative star. Tiny serif letters peeked through the torn edge.

"C—t—'s Catalog," perhaps.

A catalog.

Humans loved catalogs. They circled items, dog-eared pages, and left them lying around until someone else had to put them away.

But this one felt different. Important. Forbidden.

Clara needed to see this. Clara understood how objects whispered their secrets. Amelia could follow clues too, though she sometimes needed convincing when mess was involved. But Clara—Clara was a puzzle-solver.

Lady Grey nudged the scrap with her nose. It fluttered to the floor. She batted it, sending it skidding under the door and out into the hallway.

Perfect.

A sound made her ears prick.

Footsteps.

Slow. Careful. A human trying to be quiet. Not Amelia. Not Clara. Not Doris Finch, whose footsteps always scampered like loose gossip. Not Pike, whose heavy tread announced itself with bossy confidence.

These footsteps belonged to someone who didn't want to be noticed.

Lady Grey slipped behind the wardrobe, blending into shadow.

The footsteps paused at the doorway.

A figure stepped inside. Tall, angular, silhouette blurred by the faint hallway glow. The peppermint hit her nose before the intruder moved—a sharp, icy scent.

They wore gloves. Their hands sifted through the broken drawer quickly, methodically. Not panicked—intentional.

Searching.

Hungry.

They moved to the suitcase, rustling through it, muttering low—

too softly for even Lady Grey to decipher. Their movements were tense, efficient.

What were they trying to find?

They lifted the corner of the rug. Looked under. Came up empty.

A soft, frustrated curse slipped out.

Good.

They had missed the scrap in the hall.

Lady Grey stayed perfectly still, not so much as a whisker twitching. The intruder circled the room once more, then backed out swiftly, footsteps fading down the stairs toward the back hallway.

Lady Grey waited—one, five, ten heartbeats—then emerged.

She gave the room a final sweep with her eyes. Someone had come looking for the missing pages from Covington's catalog. Someone who already knew what to search for.

She padded into the hallway. The scrap she'd pushed out lay obediently on the carpet runner, precisely where she intended Clara to find it.

She sat.

And waited.

It did not take long.

Clara's hurried footsteps rushed up the stairs. Her face appeared at the landing, breathless, scanning the hall.

Her eyes dropped almost immediately to the scrap of paper.

Clara blinked, bent, and picked it up. "Oh. What's this? Where did this come from?"

Lady Grey blinked back.

Clara studied the scrap, turning it over. "Is this... part of a catalog?"

Lady Grey hopped onto the nearest bench and began cleaning her paw.

Clara stared at her. "You clever girl," she breathed.

Finally. Humans were slow, but they got there eventually.

She slipped the scrap into her apron and hurried down the hall. Lady Grey followed, pleased with herself.

But halfway to the stairs, she stopped.

The peppermint scent drifted faintly from the North Star Suite. Beneath it, something else whispered to her—the faint trace of something old, like ink pressed deep into paper and tucked into a cedar drawer.

Lady Grey slipped into the room one more time.

This time, she went straight to the vent near the bed.

Earlier, she'd noticed a strange hiss in the metal grate. Now she pressed her ear closer.

The heating system hummed. The wind rattled the shutters. Then—

A whisper, carried along cold metal.

"...must find... the rest..."

Lady Grey stiffened.

Another whisper, clearer this time—as if someone in a room above or below spoke directly into the ductwork.

"No one must find the rest."

Lady Grey's fur rose along her spine, tail puffing despite her best efforts to remain composed.

Someone else was listening to the walls of the inn.

Someone who knew exactly what Covington had been looking for.

Someone who did not want Amelia or Clara discovering the remaining pieces.

Lady Grey backed away from the vent with deliberate care, pupils wide and alert.

She trotted briskly toward the stairs.

Her humans needed to know.

Something in this inn had shifted tonight—changed shape like a living creature—and Lady Grey feared it would not settle again until the truth clawed its way into the light.

Chapter 5

Snowed In at the Inn

The storm did not ease—it roared.

By the time Amelia climbed down from the landing where she and Clara had inspected the forced-open suite, the windows were nearly white with swirling snow. Wind howled around the eaves, making the old beams creak in uneasy protest. Christmas lights along the porch blinked beneath a skin of frost, and the once-charming wreath on the front door thumped against the wood like an impatient visitor demanding entry.

The Tumblebrook Inn had weathered many winters, but tonight it seemed to brace itself against more than just cold.

The guests sensed it, too.

Back in the dining room, conversation had dropped to a low, troubled murmur. The wide windows showed only darkness and rushing flakes. The candles Clara had lit flickered in the drafts. Someone had tucked a blanket around Doris Finch's shoulders. Ezra hovered near the fireplace, staring into the flames as if hoping answers lay hidden in the embers.

Amelia's heart clenched.

These weren't just patrons. Many were neighbors—people she'd grown up seeing at the post office, at Doris's café, at the summer farmer's market. The inn had always been where they came for weddings and anniversaries, for quiet weekends and noisy family breakfasts.

They were looking to her now.

Trusting her.

She swallowed hard.

"Well," she said, stepping forward with the briskness expected of an innkeeper and not a woman whose hands still shook, "it looks like we're officially snowed in."

A ripple went through the room—fear mixed with resignation. The storm hammered the windows in emphatic agreement.

Alden Pike let out an exaggerated groan. "Fantastic. Trapped with a murderer in a quaint holiday postcard."

Clara shot him a warning look. "Mr. Pike, please."

Amelia rubbed her palms together, trying to gather warmth and clarity at once. "Sheriff Daniels will come as soon as the roads open," she said. "Until then, I need everyone to stay together. No wandering off alone. The weather's bad, and we need to account for where everyone is."

The guests nodded in various degrees of compliance—some fearful, some annoyed, some simply exhausted. Lady Grey leapt onto a bench by the wall and curled her tail neatly around her paws, looking for all the world like a small, judgmental chaperone presiding over unruly students.

The inn, once filled with laughter and music, now felt like a held breath.

Clara leaned close to Amelia, voice low. "We should check Covington's room again. More carefully this time. If someone broke in up there, they were looking for something."

Amelia nodded. "I'll do it. Can you keep everyone settled? Cocoa, cookies, small talk, mild intimidation?"

"Already on it," Clara said. "If anyone tries to wander, I'll assign them dish duty."

The kitchen was warm—almost too warm compared to the icy press of the storm outside. The lingering scent of cinnamon sugar clung to the air, a comforting reminder that this day had begun with nothing more sinister than holiday baking. Amelia moved through the familiar space on instinct, grabbing a flashlight and the smaller key ring she kept for guest-only possessions. The metal jingled softly as she clipped the ring to her belt. Her hands still shook around the edges.

"You've got this," she whispered to herself, though she wasn't entirely convinced.

When she reached the North Star Suite again, she paused just outside the broken frame. Snow whistled along the roof above, and the hallway lights flickered under the strain of the storm.

She pressed her palm briefly to the splintered wood.

"Okay," she murmured. "Just look. Don't touch unless you have to."

Lady Grey trotted up behind her and sat squarely in the doorway, as if keeping guard. Her steady, unblinking gaze nudged a small smile onto Amelia's face.

"Thank you, dear. But stay close, please."

The cat blinked in slow acceptance.

Amelia stepped inside.

The room felt colder than the hallway. Maybe it was the draft sneaking through the aging window frame—or maybe the echo of panic and violence left its own chill. Her gaze drifted over the open suitcase, the scattered papers, the rumpled bedspread where someone had searched frantically or fought clumsily with furniture and drawers.

Someone had been here with a plan. And not a kind one.

Her gaze snagged on Covington's coat, draped over the desk chair.

A coat was personal. People hid things in them. Receipts. Secrets.

She approached slowly, as if afraid the garment might collapse in on itself and take whatever answers it held with it. Heavy wool, charcoal gray, surprisingly soft. She patted the outer pockets: gloves, a folded pamphlet from the heritage showcase, a tin of peppermint mints emitting that sharp, clean scent she'd noticed earlier.

A strange pang tugged at her. The peppermint wasn't the intruder's signature after all—it was Covington's. A small, ordinary habit now tangled in something terrible.

She reached for the inner breast pocket.

Her fingers brushed paper.

She slid it free.

A certificate. No—several pages stapled together. Appraisal documents, the kind Covington prepared for collectors, museums, wealthy clients. She'd seen examples earlier in the year when arranging his festival duties.

She held the pages under the lamp, angling the light.

They detailed the valuation of an antique ornament—a rare hand-painted Bavarian sphere dated circa 1890, worth nearly $18,000.

Client name: Alden Pike.

Amelia blinked.

Alden Pike. The same Alden Pike now complaining loudly about being trapped in a storm. The same Alden Pike who'd been more irritated than afraid when Covington died. The same Alden Pike who seemed to bristle at every mention of inconvenience.

Her pulse skittered.

The document seemed odd in another way. She looked closer at the signature—Covington's name, looping across the bottom. It was close to what she'd seen in the guestbook.

Close—but not right.

Sharper in places. Less curved. Almost... as if someone had practiced it.

She frowned, bringing the paper even closer. In the lower corner, faint but distinct, tiny blotches of ink sat with suspicious uniformity. The kind of artificial "bleed" she'd seen on cheap reproductions—too regular to be true aging.

Printed. Smudged. Made to look older than it was.

"This is forged," she whispered.

Lady Grey meowed once, sharply, as if in agreement.

Amelia folded the papers carefully, her fingers slow with dread.

She'd hoped this weekend would be simple—hot cocoa, bright lights, children bundled in scarves. Instead, she stood in a guest room with forged documents in her hand and a dead man downstairs who might have known all about them.

She needed answers. And she needed help.

She swept the flashlight across the room one more time—no more obvious papers, no hidden catalog pages lying in plain sight. Whatever the intruder had wanted, they either hadn't found it or had already taken it.

Back in the hallway, the storm muttered against the roof. Amelia tucked the forged appraisal into the inside pocket of her cardigan, close to her heart, and headed toward the dining room.

The guests looked up as she entered—some anxious, others openly curious. The air was thick with cocoa steam and whispered theory.

Mr. Lark sat near the fireplace, spectacles perched precariously on his nose, cradling his mug of cocoa as though it were a fragile relic. When Amelia walked toward him, he straightened, one brow lifting in quiet inquiry.

"Ah," he said softly, "you've found something."

Amelia hesitated only a second. She trusted Mr. Lark—he'd been recommending mysteries and histories to her since she was old enough to reach the low shelves at Gossamer Fables. If anyone in this room understood patterns and people, it was him.

But trust tonight came with barbs.

She sat beside him, keeping her voice low. "You knew Covington's work better than most of us. Tell me what you know that isn't in the festival brochure."

Nearby guests went subtly quieter, ears stretching invisibly in their direction. Mr. Lark noticed and serenely ignored it, rotating his mug thoughtfully between his hands.

"I only met him twice," he said. "But I followed his career. The man had a reputation."

"What kind of reputation?" Amelia asked.

Mr. Lark leaned in, voice just above a whisper. "In his early years, Covington authenticated a series of rare ornaments—Victorian tears, Murano spirals, Bavarian spheres. Stunning pieces. Museums flocked to his assessments."

Amelia's fingers tightened around the hidden pages inside her pocket.

"But then," Mr. Lark continued, "questions arose. A collector in Chicago claimed a piece he authenticated was fake. Others began comparing notes. Discrepancies surfaced. A few institutions quietly withdrew their purchases. There were... legal entanglements."

"So he made mistakes?" Amelia asked.

"Perhaps," Mr. Lark said. "But a pattern of questionable pieces is difficult to pass off as simple error. Some believed he knowingly authenticated forgeries. Others insisted he was being used by someone cleverer, someone behind the scenes. Either way, his reputation cracked. He disappeared from the larger stage for a time. When he resurfaced, he kept mainly to smaller exhibits, local showcases, private clients."

Like Alden Pike.

Amelia swallowed. "Do you think he was still involved in forgery?"

Mr. Lark sighed, his shoulders drooping a little. "I think," he said carefully, "that a man who's lost his good name can become desperate to reclaim it. Desperation makes people vulnerable—to temptation and to threats."

The wind slammed against the nearest window, rattling the glass so loudly that Doris squeaked and clutched her cocoa tighter. Clara hurried over to draw the curtains, her movements purposeful, her gaze sweeping the room like a quiet headcount.

"Whatever Covington was involved in," Amelia said slowly, "someone knew. The door to his room was forced. They were looking for something."

Mr. Lark nodded. "People don't kill for nothing," he said softly. "They kill for fear, or revenge, or acquisition."

"Comforting," Amelia muttered.

He gave her an apologetic smile. "Only trying to help."

"You are," she said, standing. "Thank you."

She slipped away toward the back of the inn, Lady Grey falling into step beside her as if attached by invisible string.

The office was her sanctuary—a small room near the kitchen with deep blue walls, a heavy oak desk she'd inherited from her grand-mother, and shelves crammed full of old guest records and invoices tucked neatly into wooden boxes. A single lamp on the desk bathed everything in a soft, golden pool of light, making the storm outside feel almost distant.

Almost.

She closed the door behind her and turned the lock.

Her hands fumbled with the file drawer. She slid the forged certificate inside an empty folder and pushed it back, wanting it out of sight before the panic it carried could fully take hold.

She exhaled slowly.

This was her inn. Her responsibility. She'd kept it running through broken pipes, tourist droughts, and one memorable raccoon invasion. She could handle this.

She had to.

The door nudged inward before the latch caught. Lady Grey shouldered it open with a small but determined push, slipping inside like liquid silver. Amelia couldn't help but let out a weak laugh.

"You're relentless," she said, lifting the cat onto the desk.

Lady Grey settled immediately, paws tucked beneath her, a purring paperweight anchoring the stack of worries in place.

Amelia rubbed her eyes with the heels of her hands. "What do we do, Grey? We wait. Daniels won't arrive until morning—maybe later if the storm keeps up. We keep everyone safe. We keep things... together."

Lady Grey blinked slowly.

Amelia sank into her chair, letting her head fall back. The storm's howl grew louder, running along the roof and down the chimney like a living thing. A draft slid under the office door, cool against her ankles.

The inn creaked again—old wood shifting under strain—but something in the sound tightened her shoulders. Every familiar groan suddenly felt like a question.

Then she heard it.

Footsteps.

Soft. Deliberate. Moving outside her locked office door.

Her heart stuttered.

No one should be here. Clara was in the dining room. The guests were all gathered together, at least in theory. Ezra rarely left the hearth. Doris wasn't stealthy on her best day. Who was walking so quietly in this part of the inn?

Her breath caught.

A faint melody floated down the hall.

A soft, delicate tinkling tune.

She knew it instantly.

Covington's music box.

The one that had chimed in the parlor earlier as he'd let her wind it, explaining its origins—a delicate glass-chime lullaby, meant to echo like stars in a winter sky.

But the music box wasn't here. It had been with his belongings. With him.

The thought that it might now be in the hallway, in someone else's hand, made her blood run cold.

The melody grew clearer.

Notes chimed gently, eerily, the sound winding together with the wind through the inn's bones. It was almost pretty—almost—until you remembered the man who no longer breathed.

Lady Grey sat up, ears pricked, fur lifting along her spine.

Amelia rose slowly, quietly, each heartbeat like a fist against her ribs. She moved toward the door, the music growing louder with every careful step.

She reached for the lock.

Another soft footstep.

A shadow slid across the narrow strip of light at the bottom of the door.

Amelia froze.

The music box melody trilled its final note, a high, glassy sound that hung in the air, echoing down the hall like a ghost whispering goodnight.

Then—

Silence.

Amelia swallowed hard.

The inn was no longer just snowed in.

It was holding its secrets close.

And one of them—cold, deliberate, and very much alive—had just walked past her door.

Chapter 6

A Secret Sleigh

By the time Clara left the dining room to check on the kitchen, the wind had turned mean. It rattled the window frames in frantic pulses, as though the blizzard were clawing at the inn, searching for cracks in its cheerful façade. The old beams groaned in protest, and with every gust Clara felt the tremor all the way down to her boots.

Everyone was on edge.

Doris Finch had burst into tears over her cocoa. Ezra sat hunched by the fire like a carved gargoyle, staring at something only he could see. Alden Pike paced and muttered loudly about "liability," as though the storm and the dead man in the parlor had personally inconvenienced him. Mr. Lark watched the room with narrowed eyes, quietly tallying invisible columns.

And Amelia—dear, earnest, fraying-at-the-seams Amelia—had retreated to the office. Which meant Clara was now unofficially in charge of crowd control during a murder lockdown.

She felt the weight of it pressing down like a stack of heavy books.

Responsibility. Fear. Mystery. And somewhere beneath it all, a thin thread of determination tugging her forward.

She pushed open the swinging kitchen door and stepped into the welcome heat. Cinnamon, baked sugar, and rising dough wrapped around her like an old blanket. She took one long breath. Then another.

"Okay," she muttered. "Focus. Organize. Observe. Keep everyone alive. Preferably in that order."

The kitchen was tidy—more or less. Amelia's version of spotless allowed for a few cracks under stress. A precarious tower of mixing bowls teetered near the sink. A wooden spoon lay abandoned on the stovetop. And six gingerbread men cooled on a rack, staring up at her with sugar-crystal eyes that felt uncomfortably judgmental.

Clara grabbed a dishtowel and began wiping the counters—a ritual that always helped her think. Her mind spun through the puzzle she'd been assembling since the power flicker.

Covington clutching a shattered red ornament.

A cryptic note in his pocket.

His suite violently broken into.

A scrap of catalog—thank you, Lady Grey—mysteriously appearing in the hallway.

And Covington's frayed tension before he died, now remembered in hindsight by several guests.

Something bigger hid beneath the surface of all this. Something layered. Historical. Personal.

Her mother always said Clara didn't just remember things—she catalogued them. She sorted details like a librarian shelving secrets.

And right now, a pattern was starting to emerge.

She reached for a tray of mugs to refill them—then paused.

Cold brushed her ankles.

The pantry door was ajar.

That wasn't normal.

The pantry was insulated. Barely, yes, but enough to keep out drafts. Clara stepped over and nudged the door fully open.

She expected flour spills or rogue mice.

Instead—

A faint spark glimmered from the back corner.

Metallic. Cold. Wrong.

Clara squinted and stepped inside.

The air here was noticeably colder—like someone had cracked open a window she didn't know existed. She pushed crates aside until her hand bumped a wooden box, older than the rest.

T.B. INN – 1924

The words sprawled elegantly across the lid in fading, looping script.

Her heartbeat quickened.

Tumblebrook Inn.

1924—almost a century ago.

The same era that kept colliding with their investigations into the Monarch Society.

"What are you doing back here?" she whispered.

She tugged the crate free, dust rising in a soft, ghostly cloud, and slid the lid aside.

Inside lay a velvet box, deep forest green, its gold lettering shimmering faintly despite the age.

For the Winter Gala

A shiver threaded down her spine.

She'd read about the Winter Gala in archived newspapers—grand holiday events hosted by the Monarch Society, always exclusive, always secretive. Rich families gathered under the guise of charity, trading favors and influence behind wreath-covered doors.

Holding her breath, she lifted the lid.

Nestled within the velvet was a silver ornament shaped like a tiny sleigh.

It was exquisite—hand-carved, delicate, gleaming even in the dim pantry light. Its runners curled in graceful patterns of ivy and snowflakes. Its seat held faint traces of red enamel, cracked with age.

It wasn't just beautiful.

It was important.

She lifted it gently, feeling its cool weight settle into her palms.

Under the ornament lay a folded note.

Crisp white paper. Elegant handwriting. The same style as the tag she'd found in Covington's pocket. The same hand behind the ornament he'd died holding.

She unfolded it.

For those who steal from the past.

Her breath caught.

She read it again. And again.

For those who steal from the past.

The message wasn't just a threat. It was a judgment. A warning. A motive.

And suddenly, a horrible possibility crystallized:

What if Covington wasn't murdered because of who he was now...

...but because of what he'd uncovered from before?

She tucked the sleigh back into its velvet cradle, slid the note into her apron pocket, and pushed the crate deeper into the pantry for the moment. Her mind buzzed with connections—Monarch Society, century-old secrets, forged appraisal documents, broken ornaments with cryptic inscriptions.

Someone was crafting a narrative.

And someone else was silencing it.

Clara stepped back into the kitchen and flicked on the overhead lights. The brightness didn't help her nerves much, but at least it let her see her notebook clearly. She grabbed it from the counter and scribbled furiously:

1924 crate

Winter Gala

Silver sleigh ornament

Threatening note

Covington's forged documents

Monarch Society connection?

She snapped the notebook shut.

A knock on the swinging door made her jump.

"Clara? You back there?" Doris Finch's voice trembled through the wood.

Clara opened the door.

Doris looked miserable—cheeks blotchy, eyes wet, apron askew. Panic clung to her like lint.

Clara guided her inside. "Sit. Breathe."

Doris sank onto a stool. "I know people think Covington was arrogant, but he wasn't always like that."

"You knew him?" Clara asked softly.

Doris nodded. "Years ago. Before his name meant anything."

Clara didn't speak. Doris always told everything in her own time —especially when emotion pushed the words loose.

"My husband—Paul—got caught up in a bad art deal," Doris whispered. "Forged pieces. Expensive ones. Paul didn't know at first, but when he did... it was too late. Covington exposed the entire operation."

Clara's chest squeezed.

"He didn't do it to hurt us," Doris said, wiping her eyes. "He was doing his job. But Paul couldn't take the shame. It destroyed him."

Clara placed a hand over hers. "I'm sorry."

Doris nodded shakily. "I argued with Covington tonight because he recognized my name. I was terrified he'd bring it up. But I swear, Clara—I didn't hurt him."

"I believe you," Clara said gently.

She did. Doris's fear was too real, too raw, to be faked.

"Did you see him talking to anyone? Before the lights went out?" Clara asked.

Doris shook her head. "He was looking at the ornaments. But... he seemed nervous. Distracted. Like he felt eyes on him."

Clara's pulse quickened. "Eyes from where?"

Doris opened her mouth to answer—

A loud thump echoed from the dining room.

Ezra shouted for everyone to stay calm.

Clara shot to her feet. "Stay here. I'll check."

She hurried through the swinging door.

The dining room buzzed like a shaken hive. Ezra was righting a fallen chair. Alden Pike was dramatically bemoaning drafts. Mr. Lark stood with his arms crossed, frown deepening by the second.

Clara moved toward the window—and froze.

Outside, beyond the frosted glass, a figure stood at the edge of the trees.

Tall. Unmoving. Dark against the swirling snow.

Watching.

The moment stretched, cold and sharp as a blade.

Lady Grey leapt onto the windowsill. Her fur bristled. She hissed.

Clara blinked—

And the figure was gone.

But the dread it left behind clung to the glass like frost.

Something was out there.

And it wasn't finished.

Chapter 7

Cat on the Rafters

L ady Grey liked the attic.

Not because it was warm (it wasn't), or comfortable (it certainly wasn't), or because she was supposed to be up there (Amelia would have opinions)—but because it was *interesting*.

Humans rarely visited the space above their own heads. They walked through life blind to everything past eye level, obsessed with carpets, furniture, crumbs, and coffee cups. But the attic... the attic was for those who understood that the world had layers.

And Lady Grey understood layers.

Tonight, something called her there.

She sat at the base of the narrow staircase hidden behind the linen closet. The place smelled of cedar, dust, and the faintest thread of pine resin—sharp, fresh, and entirely out of place. Pine resin belonged downstairs, on the Christmas tree. Not up here.

Which meant someone had carried it upward.

Lady Grey placed one paw on the first step. Then the next. The wooden treads creaked faintly under her small weight, whispering secrets into the dark. The higher she climbed, the colder the air grew, as though the storm outside had slid its fingers through the roof and latched onto the beams.

She was not afraid.

The attic hatch was already ajar.

Interesting.

Amelia would never leave it that way.

Lady Grey nudged it with her head. The wood swung open with a soft groan, and she slipped inside.

The attic stretched out like a cavern of forgotten memories. Boxes stacked three high. Old suitcases arranged like awkward guests. A broken rocking horse missing an eye. Coils of rope. A trunk with brass hinges. A musty armchair with lace doilies still pinned to its back, as if expecting a visitor who never arrived.

Lady Grey took it all in—every scent, every draft, every shifting shadow.

The pine smell grew stronger.

She followed it across the floorboards, stepping lightly so her movement made little more than a whisper. Dust motes drifted around her like tiny stars. The wind pressed against the roof, causing a beam to groan, then settle.

She passed a nest of old wreaths and garlands, their fake berries dulled with age. A dried sprig of cinnamon tied with a faded ribbon caught her attention; she sniffed it once, cataloging the scent for future relevance. Humans had stored that here long ago—perhaps when Amelia was still a child padding through the halls in fuzzy socks. Perhaps even earlier, when Amelia's grandmother ruled the inn with stern grace and soft hands.

The attic was full of ghosts, but not the kind that frightened Lady Grey.

These ghosts were memories.

Warm ones.

She moved on.

The pine resin scent deepened. Beneath it now came something else—varnish. Fresh varnish, pungent and sharp, as though someone had been sealing wood within the last day or two.

Her ears pricked.

She wove around a stack of crates. One brushed her flank and rocked slightly. Something inside jangled—a faint, brittle music.

Glass.

Ornaments.

Lady Grey paused. Curiosity flared. She pressed her paw against the crate lid. The wood lifted just enough for dust to puff outward. That was all she needed. She slid her head beneath.

Inside was a nest of straw and cloth. Nestled within were ornaments—old ones. Silver bells. Painted wooden soldiers. Tarnished globes whose colors had faded into dreamy half-memories. Their hooks tangled in the fabric like sleeping birds' claws.

But at the front of the crate, where the straw formed a shallow hollow, there was an empty space.

A missing slot.

Lady Grey leaned closer. Beneath the hollow, carved faintly into the crate's base, was a small symbol: twin wings unfurled in mid-flicker, symmetrical and stylized.

A butterfly.

Her fur rose along her spine.

The same Monarch butterfly emblem she had seen before—hidden in other corners of the inn when secrets stirred. The mark of that whisper-spun society tied to Tumblebrook's past.

Lady Grey sniffed the empty hollow. The scent confirmed it: pine, varnish... and that faint peppermint that had threaded through the inn since Covington arrived. Not sharp like the tin in his pocket—fainter, ghostlike.

Someone had taken that ornament recently.

Her whiskers quivered.

She backed out of the crate and stepped lightly onto a wooden beam that cut across the attic like a catwalk built just for her. She climbed onto it, settling into a low crouch to survey the space from above.

Her tail froze mid-swish.

Movement.

A shadow that didn't belong to dust or rafters or the wavering branches outside the tiny attic window.

A human—moving quickly.

Lady Grey's pupils widened, catching the slight shift in texture between darkness and a darker shape. Someone stood near the trapdoor.

She flattened herself along the beam and watched.

A boot heel scraped wood. A muffled grunt. A breath caught tight in a human throat.

The footsteps were hurried. Retreating.

Not the measured tread of someone exploring.

Someone startled.

Disturbed.

Fleeing.

Lady Grey's fur puffed despite her best efforts at composure.

The figure vanished down the stairs. The attic hatch thumped shut with a soft, decisive sound.

She was alone again.

Alone with the swirling dust, the missing ornament slot, and the carved Monarch emblem that seemed to stare back at her.

She needed to leave something behind—something humans would understand. A breadcrumb. A trail. A clue.

Lady Grey hopped off the beam and padded toward the trapdoor.

There—on the floor near the opening—something small glinted in the lamplight seeping up from the stairwell. She bent her head and sniffed.

Not glass. Not metal. Softer. Warmer. Human.

A button.

A coat button.

She nudged it with her nose, testing its weight. Round. Smooth.

Lighter than it appeared. And beneath the dust and attic air, she caught a familiar scent:

Peppermint.

Paper.

Ink.

Wool.

Covington.

Lady Grey nudged the button again, then gave it a firm swipe. It rolled toward the hatch and dropped neatly down the top stair with a tiny, satisfying *plink*.

Good.

Humans were blind to the important things, but they understood dropped objects. Especially dropped objects with letters scratched into them.

She followed at a dignified pace, stepping carefully down the steep stairs. The button came to rest on the landing, right where attentive eyes would fall.

Lady Grey sat beside it, tail wrapped around her paws, and waited.

Below, voices rose and fell—muffled, anxious. The storm clawed at the walls, rattling the siding like impatient fingers on a locked door.

The inn groaned—a deep, tired sound.

A draft slipped along the hallway floor, curling around Lady Grey's whiskers.

She didn't like drafts. They were sneaky. Cold. Rude.

But this draft carried scent.

Peppermint.

Again.

She issued a tiny, dignified growl—a rumble more than a sound. Peppermint now meant trouble. Peppermint meant Covington. Peppermint meant whoever had been where they shouldn't be—the North Star Suite. The attic.

She nudged the button into an even more prominent spot on the landing, exactly where Clara's quick eyes would land.

Clara was the quickest. Clara asked questions. Clara noticed what was out of place.

Lady Grey approved of Clara.

Footsteps echoed from the stairs below—two sets. Clara's lighter tread. Amelia's more hurried one. Their voices floated up, urgent and frayed.

Of course something else had happened.

Chaos traveled in packs.

Clara reached the landing first. Lady Grey gave a soft, authoritative *mrrrp*.

Clara stopped.

Her gaze dropped. "Oh," she breathed. She bent and lifted the button between thumb and forefinger. "What's this doing up here?"

She turned it over.

Two engraved letters caught the light, faint but unmistakable:

E.C.

Edward Covington.

Clara's breath hitched. "Is this off his coat?"

Amelia hurried up, hair a little wild from stress and the storm. "What is it—Clara, what did you find?"

Clara held out the button. "It was on the floor. Right beside Lady Grey. She... left it for us."

Lady Grey flicked her tail, satisfied with the acknowledgement she already knew she deserved.

Amelia squinted, her expression tightening. "This must have come from his room."

"No," Clara said slowly. "If it was in his room, it wouldn't be up here now." She turned the button in her fingers. "This came off whoever was wearing his coat—or handling it—after he died."

Amelia's eyes widened.

Lady Grey sat with regal composure while the humans finally began to catch up.

Clara angled the button toward the hallway light. Something else glinted on the metal edge—just a whisper of a mark, almost lost under years of wear.

"Wait," she murmured. "There's something else."

She held her breath and tilted it.

There—so faint it was almost a suggestion rather than an engraving—spread a tiny pair of wings in a delicate arc.

A butterfly.

A Monarch butterfly.

Lady Grey's ears flattened.

The storm raged outside. The inn creaked and shifted. Somewhere below, a window rattled in its frame.

The past was not just alive.

It was circling.

And it had just left its calling card in the rafters.

Chapter 8

Tinsel and Tensions

If someone had told Amelia Farnsworth a week earlier that she would be hosting cocoa night during a blizzard—with a murder victim lying under a sheet in the adjacent parlor—she would have laughed. Politely. Awkwardly. The kind of brittle laugh reserved for holiday parties when someone jokes about family drama.

But tonight wasn't a party.

It was survival.

And the best tools she had were cocoa, cookies, and firelight.

She moved through the dining room with the steady grace of an innkeeper who had spent years smoothing ruffled feathers. She refilled mugs from the large enamel pot Clara had set on a trivet, making sure everyone got precisely what they needed—Doris Finch liked too many marshmallows, Alden Pike none at all, Mr. Lark exactly three, and Ezra a single one that he stared at like a tiny snow-covered omen.

People calmed down when their hands were warm.

That was Amelia's theory, anyway.

The storm shrieked around the inn, rattling the shutters and sneaking icy drafts under doorframes, but inside the dining room the fire crackled and nervous conversations drifted through the air like fragile steam.

Amelia tried to project calm, but inside she felt like a wind-up toy —gears wound too tight, one jostle away from snapping.

Doris Finch clutched her mug as if it were a life preserver. "It's the weather's fault," she whispered hoarsely. "Blizzards during festivities are bad luck. Always have been."

Across the long farmhouse table, Alden Pike snorted. "This is Minnesota, Doris. Snow happens. You can't blame the weather for..." He jerked his chin toward the parlor doorway. "...for *that*."

"I didn't say the blizzard killed him," Doris snapped. "But storms stir up old energies. Everyone knows that."

"No," Alden said pointedly, "everyone does *not* know that."

Amelia stepped between them with a practiced smile. "Let's keep things friendly, please. Tensions are high, and we're all stuck here together until morning."

Alden crossed his arms. "Not your fault, Amelia, but this is a nightmare. Roads closed. Power flickering. Phones barely working. And now a killer—"

"We don't know that," Amelia said, though she heard the doubt in her own voice.

She couldn't allow panic to take root. Fear spread faster than cold.

Lady Grey perched on a chair nearby, tail tucked neatly around her paws, looking every bit the tiny, furry judge presiding over the room. When Alden complained too loudly, she narrowed her amber eyes at him.

Alden blinked. "I... wasn't yelling at the cat."

"Lady Grey dislikes raised voices," Amelia said smoothly. "So does everyone else."

A murmur of agreement drifted through the room. Alden, flustered, reached for a cookie.

Amelia made a mental note to reward Lady Grey later.

She checked on Ezra, who stared into his cocoa as if reading the future in the reflection of his single marshmallow.

"How are you holding up, Ezra?" she asked.

He looked up sharply, wild eyebrows bristling. "Strange winds tonight. Strange sounds. They blow through the trees wrong."

"The storm is unsettling," Amelia said gently. "But we're safe in here."

"Hm."

He sipped his cocoa. The marshmallow stuck to his beard.

Amelia hesitated. Ezra was odd, yes, but usually not this tightly wound. Something tugged at him—something he hadn't yet decided whether to share.

"Ezra," she said softly, "if you know something... anything... now would be the time."

His grip tightened on his mug.

"Covington," he murmured. "He came to my cabin last week."

Amelia's breath caught. "He did?"

"Showed up before dusk. Strange fellow. Always looking at things sideways, like truth reshaped itself every time the light shifted."

Amelia eased onto the bench beside him. "What did he want?"

"He asked about the legend."

A cold knot tightened in her stomach. "What legend?"

Ezra blinked, surprised she didn't know. "The ornament. The one said to be hidden in these woods. Priceless. Secret. Passed down through private hands."

Her grandmother's stories flitted through her memory—tales of a Monarch Society Christmas gala, an ornament that "went wrong," whispers of silence and scandal.

"Ezra," she asked quietly, "what did Covington want with it?"

"He said someone was trying to find it first," Ezra said, glancing toward the dark windows. "Someone dangerous."

A chill slipped down Amelia's spine.

"Did you tell him anything?"

"I told him legends are legends." Ezra shook his head. "Doesn't stop men from digging where they shouldn't."

The fire cracked loudly behind them. Ezra flinched.

Before Amelia could ask more, Alden Pike's voice cut through the room.

"This entire night is a disaster!"

Amelia exhaled sharply. "Excuse me."

Clara intercepted her halfway, carrying the empty cocoa pot like a shield. "Alden is reaching peak melodrama. Do you want him, or should I run interference?"

"You take Alden," Amelia said. "He respects you more than he knows."

Clara smirked—then Alden stomped over.

"This is ridiculous," he said, red-cheeked. "We should be evacuating or forming a plan or *something!* The man was murdered!"

"Lower your voice," Clara said. "You're upsetting people."

"People *should* be upset! We're trapped! What if the killer is still here?"

Lady Grey hopped onto the table, tail puffing just enough to make a point.

Alden froze. "I wasn't yelling at the cat."

"She's aware," Clara murmured.

The room settled slightly. Amelia took a steadying breath.

She needed to keep them together. Calm. Focused.

She stepped into the center of the room.

"All right, everyone," she said softly, "thank you for your patience. I know this is frightening. But we're going to get through this together. We'll stay warm, stay close, and look out for one another. The inn is sturdy, even if the storm is loud."

Doris wiped her eyes. "Your grandmother would know what to do."

Amelia's heart squeezed. "My grandmother would've made more cocoa. Or pulled out a box of cookies and put everyone to work decorating."

56

A few chuckles lifted the tension.

"She always said, 'When the world feels too big, make your home feel small,'" Amelia added. "So that's what we're doing. Staying close. No wandering off alone."

She almost added *and stay away from the upstairs hallway,* but decided against sparking unwanted curiosity.

She raised the cocoa pot. "Refills?"

A forest of hands rose.

As she poured, her mind churned.

The silver sleigh Clara had found.

The notes with ominous messages.

The missing attic ornament.

The Monarch butterfly emblem.

Ezra's legend.

Covington's obsession.

Her grandmother's old story whispered in the back of her mind:

A missing ornament.

A ruined gala.

A silence no one dared break.

She stepped toward the table to refill another mug when—

The lights flickered.

Once.

Twice.

Then steadied.

Guests murmured uneasily.

"Probably the wind," Amelia said, though dread pooled in her stomach.

She turned back to the cocoa pot—

The lights flickered again.

Longer this time.

The fire threw giant shadows onto the walls. The room seemed to inhale.

Then—

Darkness.

A scream.

A shattering mug.

Someone grabbed Amelia's arm.

"Stay calm!" she called. "The generator—"

Before she finished, the lights blasted back on.

Bright. Too bright.

Then normal.

The room gasped in unison.

Amelia turned to reassure everyone—and froze.

The parlor display case.

Where she had arranged her grandmother's ornaments earlier.

It stood wide open.

Empty.

Every ornament.

Every heirloom.

Gone.

"No," Amelia whispered, stumbling forward. "No, no, no..."

Clara rushed to her. "Amelia?"

Guests crowded behind them, panic rising again.

The display doors hung crooked, their hinges twisted. Velvet-lined shelves were bare except for a faint scatter of dust where something had been hastily swept away.

Lady Grey jumped onto the empty case, tail lashing, sniffing the hollow space with slow, furious precision.

Someone had used the blackout.

Someone had taken everything.

"Who would do this?" Doris sobbed.

"This isn't just murder," Alden growled. "This is a setup. Someone's playing a game."

Ezra murmured a prayer under his breath.

Amelia could barely breathe.

Her grandmother's ornaments—gone.

Covington's clues—gone.

The legend—very much alive.

The Monarch Society was no longer a whisper.

It was a shadow moving through her inn.

Everyone turned at the same moment.

A faint sound drifted down the hallway leading to the stairs.

A clink.

A soft scrape.

The unmistakable tap of metal against glass.

Something—or someone—was still inside the inn.

And it was moving.

Amelia's heart slammed against her ribs.

"Everyone," she said, voice trembling, "stay together."

But even as she spoke, she felt it:

The past hadn't just crept in.

It had been waiting.

Chapter 9

A Trail of Notes

Clara did not sleep.

Even after Amelia walked the last guest to their room and checked the locks twice, even after Lady Grey curled on her pillow and rumbled a soothing purr, even after Clara told herself—sternly—that worrying wouldn't change anything, she lay awake and listened.

The storm battered the inn like an angry visitor demanding entry.

Wind moaned through the eaves.

A shutter thumped a broken rhythm.

Somewhere in the walls, the heat pipes hummed their tense metallic song.

And beneath all that, Clara sensed something else.

Movement.

Soft.

Stealthy.

Human.

By "morning"—a generous word for the sky's murky charcoal gray—she finally gave up. Lady Grey stretched luxuriously, hopped off the bed as if to say *finally*, and padded to the door.

The hallway was dim, lit only by sconces that flickered under the strain of the storm. The air smelled of burnt dust from overworked heaters and—again, unsettlingly—peppermint.

Clara paused outside Amelia's door.

Silence.

Good. Let her sleep. At least one of them should.

Clara turned toward the staircase—and froze.

Something white lay on the floor.

Small. Rectangular.

A gift tag.

The same kind Covington had carried.

Clara knelt and picked it up between careful fingers. Elegant looping handwriting swept across the front, unmistakable now that she'd seen it more than once:

For those who trade hearts for gold.

Her breath caught.

She flipped the tag over. Blank. No name, no signature.

Just judgment.

She straightened slowly—then noticed another tag near Mr. Lark's door.

A third near Alden Pike's.

A fourth near Ezra's.

A fifth near Doris Finch's.

Like breadcrumbs.

Or accusations.

Clara's stomach dipped as understanding slid into place.

Someone had walked the hallway while everyone slept, slipping these under each door. Someone quiet. Someone with access.

Lady Grey sniffed the nearest tag, tail twitching in displeasure.

Clara gathered them, one by one, until she held a small stack of six:

For those who trade hearts for gold
For those who forget their promises
For those who chase what is not theirs

For those who bury truth beneath winter
For those who break what cannot be replaced
For those who hide behind silver lies

Same graceful handwriting. Same unsettling precision.

"Okay," she whispered. "This is officially terrifying."

Lady Grey meowed crisply in agreement.

Amelia needed to see these. But waking her with nothing but fear and a handful of ominous tags felt wrong. Clara wanted context—something to stand on first.

She tucked the tags into her apron pocket and padded down the stairs, Lady Grey keeping pace.

The parlor fire had burned to embers—just a low orange glow beneath a blanket of ash. Shadows pooled across the floor like spilled ink. The ornament display case loomed on the far wall, doors yawning open, shelves stripped bare.

Empty.

She forced herself past it.

In the dining room, the early light was thin and blue. Mr. Lark sat at the table with a teapot, spectacles perched high on his forehead, reading a book that looked older than the inn itself.

He looked up the moment she appeared. "Clara. Awake early... or did you never sleep?"

"Both," she said, sinking into the chair opposite him. Lady Grey hopped up beside her, silent and alert.

He studied her face. "What happened?"

Clara laid the stack of gift tags between them.

His eyebrows shot up. "My word."

"I found them under every guest door," she said. "Each with a different phrase."

He picked one up carefully. "*For those who bury truth beneath winter.*" He hummed. "That's... dramatic."

"It's ominous," Clara corrected.

He inclined his head. "Quite."

She spread them out, the ink forming a wreath of accusations across the table.

"The handwriting," she added. "It matches the tag in Covington's pocket. And the note in the sleigh ornament box."

Mr. Lark tapped the edge of a card. "These read like... verdicts."

"I thought so too," Clara murmured.

"For whom?" he asked.

"For everyone," she whispered. "Whoever wrote these isn't just sending messages. They're accusing."

He folded his hands, gaze turning thoughtful. "Clara... how much do you know about the Monarch Society's history with ornaments?"

She blinked. "You told us about their galas. The missing ornament. The rumors. Not much more."

"That's because it's not an easy topic to discuss over tea and light fiction," he said dryly. Then, more solemnly, "Long before your grandmother's tenure, the Monarch Society used handcrafted ornaments as a kind of... code."

"Code?" Clara frowned.

"Promises. Favors. Debts." His voice dropped. "Decorative to most, but to those who knew the language, each ornament represented a transaction. A secret. A bond."

Clara stared at the tags. "Because paper can be burned."

"Exactly." He nodded. "But a code hidden in glass or metal hangs innocently on a tree for decades."

Her mind raced.

"The missing ornaments from the display case..." she said slowly.

"If they belonged to that original Monarch collection," Mr. Lark said, "someone may be trying to reclaim—or erase—the past. Or expose it."

"And Covington?" Clara asked, voice low.

"Covington authenticated rare pieces," he replied. "If he rediscovered the meanings embedded in one ornament—if he could read the old code—he could make enemies without realizing it."

"Enemies who might kill to keep those secrets buried," she finished.

Silence settled. Outside, the wind seemed to pause and listen.

"So the ornaments weren't just valuable," Clara said. "They were... evidence."

"In the right—or wrong—hands," Mr. Lark said softly, "yes."

Clara stared at the table, nausea curling in her stomach. "And these tags?" she asked, brushing her fingertips across the nearest phrase. "They're not just creepy notes, are they?"

"They could be warnings," he said. "Or threats. Or clues mimicking the old Monarch practice. But either way, whoever left them knows far more than they're saying."

"And they're inside the inn," Clara whispered.

He followed her gaze toward the parlor. "It would appear so."

Her pulse quickened.

They needed to go through Covington's belongings again—slowly, methodically—with this new context. And Amelia needed to know about the figure Clara had seen at the tree line last night, watching the inn.

Before she could speak, the kitchen door swung open.

Ezra shuffled in, coat clutched around him like a shawl, hair even more unruly than usual.

"Morning," he murmured.

Clara studied him. "Rough night?"

"Storm," Ezra grunted. "Storm and... something else."

"What else?" Mr. Lark asked.

Ezra stared at the window. "A sound. Like a whistle. Or a call. Might've been the wind trying to talk. Might've been something else listening."

Clara didn't like that answer one bit.

Lady Grey hopped onto the table, sniffed Ezra's sleeve, and sneezed.

Ezra frowned. "Bless me?"

"That," Clara muttered, "was a sneeze of suspicion."

Before he could respond, Doris Finch shuffled in—robe askew, curlers crooked, eyes glassy.

"Does anyone know why there was a little card under my door?" she asked. "I thought it was... festive. Then I read it."

Clara slid the appropriate tag toward her—***For those who break what cannot be replaced***—and handed her a mug of cocoa.

Doris read it. Her face crumpled. "Oh."

"It doesn't mean it's about you," Clara said gently. "We don't know what any of them mean yet. We'll figure it out."

Mr. Lark patted her shoulder, but Clara's mind was already racing again.

The notes.

The sleigh.

The missing attic ornament.

The Monarch emblem.

Covington's forged appraisal naming Alden Pike.

The button with Covington's initials—and the butterfly.

The watcher at the tree line.

This wasn't random.

The inn wasn't just caught in a snowstorm.

It was caught in someone else's plan.

Clara rose abruptly. "I need to talk to Amelia."

Lady Grey hopped down immediately, tail high, as if she'd been waiting for that decision.

The storm pressed against the windows, wind curling around the inn like a restless spirit. The hallway felt charged—humming with the same unease as a held breath.

Clara rounded the corner into the parlor—

—and froze.

A scream tore through the inn, sharp as broken glass.

Not distant.

Not imagined.

Now.

Pained. Real.

A body lay crumpled on the parlor floor beside the fireplace.

For a heartbeat, everything narrowed—firelight, carpet, unmoving limbs.

Clara's breath hitched. "No—"

Lady Grey hissed, fur puffed to twice her size.

Clara lunged forward, heart pounding so loudly it drowned out the wind. "Amelia!" she shouted. "Amelia, hurry—someone's down!"

Christmas lights flickered along the garlands.

The storm wailed outside.

And inside the Tumblebrook Inn, the mystery deepened— shadows pooling at Clara's feet like a second storm gathering indoors.

Chapter 10

Whiskers and Whispers

L ady Grey did not rush.

Rushing was for humans—the frantic, stumbling creatures who flung themselves toward disaster with loud footsteps and poorly timed gasps. Cats approached trouble differently.

With silence.

With calculation.

With elegance.

So when Clara's scream sliced through the inn—sharp enough to rattle the ornaments still clinging to the branches—Lady Grey did not bolt the way Clara had.

She glided.

Her paws made no sound as she slipped into the parlor, weaving between the legs of gathered guests. Humans clustered around the fireplace like panicked birds, their voices overlapping in anxious, flustered chirps.

On the floor lay Doris Finch, groaning softly while Amelia knelt beside her.

Lady Grey paused in the doorway, whiskers twitching.

Doris was conscious. Breathing. Embarrassed more than injured.

Humans always underestimated how easily fear could topple them.

Lady Grey dismissed the scene with a single flick of her ear.

Something else tugged at her senses.

A scent.

Wrong.

Burning.

The hairs along her spine lifted.

She stepped deeper into the parlor, ignoring Amelia's firm, "Stay back, Grey," because Amelia's authority was conditional, and Lady Grey respected it only when convenient.

The parlor smelled of stress and cinnamon and melted marshmallow—but beneath all of that, something darker curled through the air.

Smoke.

Acrid. Sharp.

Fresh.

Her gaze snapped toward the hearth.

A toppled candle lay on its side, its wick still smoldering. A thin ribbon of smoke drifted upward. The garland draped across the mantel—pine needles, ribbon, holly berries—had a section singed black.

One inch farther and the whole mantel could have gone up in flames.

Lady Grey lowered her nose and sniffed the scorched pine.

Burnt resin.

The same scent she'd picked up in the attic.

Her tail flicked. Whatever had burned upstairs was connected to what had almost burned here.

She swept her whiskers along the floorboards.

There—tucked behind the fallen candle.

A corner of paper.

No—a small envelope.

Lady Grey slid her claws in just enough to hook the edge and drag it out. The humans were too busy with Doris to notice anything smaller than their own panic.

Good. Panic made them blind to important things.

She nudged the envelope. It gaped open, and a sepia photograph fluttered onto the rug.

Lady Grey froze.

Not visibly—freezing visibly was undignified.

But internally, her breath stilled.

The photograph showed Amelia's grandmother, Esther Farnsworth, standing before a towering Christmas tree dripping with shimmering ornaments. Even in black-and-white, they gleamed with the intricate metalwork Lady Grey recognized.

The Monarch Gala tree.

Clara and Amelia had whispered about it often enough. Lady Grey had listened, as she always did, from warm nests on quilts and bookshelves. A fateful gala. An ornament that vanished. A night no one spoke of again.

And there, unmistakable in Esther's hand, was a small silver sleigh ornament.

Matching the one Clara found in the pantry box.

Matching the empty indentation Lady Grey had seen in the attic crate.

Matching the shape missing from the black box hidden in the inn.

Lady Grey blinked slowly.

This was proof. Memory. Motive.

She nudged the photograph forward, positioning it where Clara would spot it the moment she stopped fussing over Doris.

Clues were wasted on most humans, but Clara understood patterns.

A new scent drifted past Lady Grey's nose.

Alden Pike.

Her lip curled. She did not like Pike. He smelled like expensive leather and bad decisions wrapped in artificial pine. Trouble clung to him like static.

His scent trail led out of the parlor, down the hallway toward the guest corridor.

Lady Grey followed.

Not because she was afraid.

Because she distrusted him.

And Lady Grey never ignored her instincts.

The corridor was dim, a wash of gray morning light leaking through frosted windows. The storm outside pressed against the glass like a restless animal. Inside, everything felt muted, expectant.

Lady Grey reached Pike's door and sniffed the gap beneath it.

Strong. Sharp. Wrong.

She nudged the door.

It creaked open.

He'd left in a hurry.

Lady Grey slipped inside.

The room was chaos—clothes strewn across the bed, papers scattered on the desk, suitcase half-zipped. Humans called this "organizing under pressure." Cats recognized it as "attempting to hide something poorly."

Lady Grey padded to the open suitcase.

She sniffed.

Paper. Ink. Glue. A faint metallic tang.

Secrets.

She tugged the zipper flap with her paws. It didn't budge. She tried again. Still nothing.

She sat, tail curled around her paws, and considered.

Then she applied more enthusiasm.

A forceful double-swat sent the suitcase toppling sideways.

It popped open.

Papers spilled out in a small avalanche of guilt.

Lady Grey leaned in.

These weren't travel papers or itineraries or anything reasonable.

They were legal documents.

She nudged the top page.

TRANSFER OF OWNERSHIP – TUMBLEBROOK INN

Her whiskers quivered.

She nudged another.

PROPERTY ACQUISITION – F. ESTHER FARNSWORTH ESTATE

A third:

SIGNATURE VERIFICATION – DISCREPANCY NOTED

A fourth:

DEED REVISION PROPOSAL – A. PIKE

Lady Grey hissed softly.

Forgeries.

The paper smelled too new. The ink too sharp. The signatures too perfect. And all of them connected to her home.

Her fur rose along her spine.

She pawed the pages harder, spreading them across the carpet like scattered accusations.

A folded sheet slipped loose and fluttered farther out.

Lady Grey opened it with careful taps of her paw.

The Monarch Society emblem stared back at her—a butterfly with wings spread.

Her heart thumped.

Below it—Covington's signature.

Except not his signature. Not exactly. The same imitation she'd scented on the appraisal.

Pike was tied to Covington.

And to the ornaments.

And to the inn.

Lady Grey's tail lashed once.

There were answers buried in Pike's suitcase. Answers humans needed.

She began methodically batting the forged documents into the hallway, forming a neat little trail. Human breadcrumb logic. They wouldn't miss this.

Satisfied, she turned back—

And stopped.

At the very bottom of the suitcase sat a small black velvet box.

She approached cautiously.

It smelled dusty-old and freshly-handled all at once. Something hidden for years, recently disturbed.

She nudged the lid.

It opened.

Inside was—

An empty ornament hook.

But the indentation beneath it was unmistakable.

A sleigh-shaped hollow.

Lady Grey's breath stilled.

So Pike had possessed the sleigh.

Or one of the sleighs.

And now it was missing.

Footsteps sounded in the hallway.

Lady Grey darted behind the dresser, fur standing on end.

A shadow paused at the doorway.

Listened.

Sniffed.

Then moved on.

Silence seeped back in.

Lady Grey padded to the suitcase again, nudged the velvet box closed, and stepped into the hallway beside her carefully arranged trail of damning paperwork.

Someone would find this soon.

Clara always followed where Lady Grey led.

Lady Grey sat proudly in the doorway, tail wrapped in perfect poise.

Alden Pike wasn't just annoying.

He was dangerous.

And he was hiding secrets sharp enough to cut through the walls of the inn.

Chapter 11

Secrets Beneath the Tree

For several long, suspended heartbeats, Amelia couldn't move.

She stood rooted beside the parlor hearth, breath catching on the frayed edges of disbelief as she stared at the sepia photograph Clara held—a frozen portrait from another lifetime. Her grandmother, Esther Farnsworth, stood elegantly beside a towering Christmas tree glittering with ornaments that somehow shimmered even through monochrome grain.

The Monarch Society tree.

The tree of town legend.

The tree she'd always assumed lived only in whispered café gossip and the embellished memories of old-timers who liked their stories served warm.

But there was Esther—young, bright-eyed, composed—resting her hand on the very silver sleigh ornament Clara had found hours earlier in the century-old pantry crate.

The floor seemed to tilt beneath Amelia.

Clara placed a steadying hand on her shoulder. "Hey. Talk to me. Are you okay?"

"I... I'm not sure," Amelia breathed.

Her grandmother had never spoken of being involved with the Monarch Society. She'd mentioned them only in cryptic asides—*Old families keep older secrets,* or *Some stories shouldn't be dusted off*—but never once hinted she had stood beside the Society's infamous holiday display. Never once hinted she had been part of something steeped in secrecy.

Amelia swallowed hard.

"I need to see that up close," she whispered.

She carried the photograph to the dining room table. Clara followed in quiet understanding. Lady Grey hopped onto the table, curling neatly beside the frame, golden eyes glowing with investigative approval.

Amelia turned the picture over.

Only a date, faint in pencil:

1924 Winter Gala

And beneath it, initials barely visible:

E.F.

"That's her handwriting," Amelia murmured. "The same loops she used on recipes... and shopping lists... and everything."

Clara leaned closer. "Do you think she hid this intentionally?"

Amelia hesitated. "She hid *something*. That much I know."

She slid a thumb along the back of the frame—and paused.

A ridge.

A seam.

A narrow divide that shouldn't exist.

Her heartbeat tripped.

"Clara—grab me a butter knife."

Clara blinked. "You're taking this seriously."

"Very."

Clara returned moments later. Amelia slid the knife into the seam and gently pried. The wooden panel popped free.

Something small and metal tumbled into Amelia's lap with a soft **clink**.

A key.

Brass, ornate, delicate—pretty enough to be decorative, but solid with purpose.

Lady Grey leaned in for a dignified sniff, then fixed Amelia with a look that clearly said: *Well? Get on with it.*

Clara raised an eyebrow. "What on earth does that open?"

"There's only one drawer in this entire inn I've never been able to open," Amelia whispered. "In my grandmother's old study. The tiny one on the left."

"You never asked her about it?"

"She always brushed it off. Said it held 'nothing worth remembering.'"

Clara snorted. "Amelia, she just hid a key inside a Monarch gala photo. I doubt it's nothing."

Amelia was already halfway down the hall.

Clara hurried after her. Lady Grey trotted alongside with purposeful little steps, tail held high like a flag leading a parade of secrets.

The old study greeted them with a hush—deep blue walls, the heavy oak desk beneath the window, the lingering scent of cedar and ink. Esther Farnsworth lived in this room still. In the grooves along the desk. In the quiet.

Amelia knelt before the narrow drawer. It looked plain. Seamless. Innocent.

She slid the brass key into the tiny hidden keyhole.

It turned with a smooth, decisive **click**.

Her breath hitched.

Slowly—almost reverently—she pulled the drawer open.

Inside lay a bundle of letters tied with a faded blue ribbon. The paper glowed ivory with age. They smelled faintly of lavender and cedar and ink pressed deep into old fibers.

Amelia lifted the top envelope.

On the front, in her grandmother's unmistakable script:

To be read only if the ornaments return to the inn.

Clara inhaled sharply. "Read it."

Amelia slid the letter free.

Winter Gala, 1924

My dearest Amelia—

She froze.

Not addressed to her—addressed to another Amelia, generations back. The Farnsworths were a family tree full of repeating names and knotted branches.

She forced herself to continue.

The Monarch Society believes the crown ornament remains lost. They are wrong. It is only hidden. Hidden for protection, not profit.

The crown carries danger. A curse, some say. But I believe the danger lies in the secrets woven into its metal—agreements made in shadows, promises bartered like coin. If uncovered, these truths will unravel more than reputations. They will unravel the town itself.

Do not return the ornament unless Tumblebrook is ready—unless those who would use it for greed are gone, and the truth can do more good than harm.

Keep it hidden. Keep it safe. Keep silent.

—E.F.

Amelia lowered the letter, throat tight.

"My grandmother hid the crown ornament," she whispered. "She hid it because she believed it was dangerous."

Clara scanned the letter again. "She wasn't just part of the Monarch Society. She was protecting people from them."

Lady Grey placed a solemn paw on the stack of letters, as though acknowledging their weight.

Amelia reached for a second envelope.

Someone has begun searching again. They sniff through the inn's corners like wolves. The Monarchs crumble under greed. If I am gone before the truth surfaces, whoever finds these must choose the right path. Secrets have a way of finding new guardians.

Before she could process the words, a heavy knock pounded through the front hall.

Amelia jumped; Clara stiffened; Lady Grey's fur spiked.

Alden Pike's voice split the quiet.

"Amelia! We need to talk. Now."

Amelia winced. "Not now. Please—not today."

They stepped into the hall to find Alden pacing deep grooves into the rug, jaw clenched, eyes wild.

"This is absurd," he snapped. "I demand to leave. I don't care about your lockdown—"

"You can't leave," Amelia cut in, injecting steel into her voice. "The bridge washed out. The roads are closed."

"Someone will come!"

"Not until the storm passes," Clara said. "Sit down, Mr. Pike. You're not helping."

He opened his mouth—probably to insult someone—when the lights flickered.

Once.

Twice.

The hallway dimmed like a pulse giving out.

Silence wrapped the inn.

Alden swallowed hard. "I—fine. Fine." He spun on his heel and stormed off toward the dining room.

Clara let out a tight breath. "His nerves are shot."

"No," Amelia murmured. "He's hiding something."

"And now we know your grandmother was hiding something too," Clara said gently.

Amelia wrapped her arms around herself. "I need time to think."

Clara nodded—and stepped back.

That's when it slid under the study door.

A thin rectangle.

A gift tag.

Amelia's stomach dropped.

She reached for it with trembling fingers.

Same elegant handwriting.

Same deliberate ink.

Same cold intent.

You are next to forget.

Amelia stumbled back.

Clara swore softly.

Lady Grey growled—low, protective.

The storm clawed at the windows, howling like something alive.

Someone wasn't just sending warnings.

They were choosing targets.

And whoever had slipped that note beneath the door...

...was close enough to touch the inn's heartbeat.

Close enough to know what Amelia feared.

Close enough to intend her harm.

Amelia gripped the tag, breath shallow.

Someone inside the inn wanted her terrified.

Someone inside the inn wanted her next.

Chapter 12

The Baker's Burden

Morning crept into the Tumblebrook Inn like a wary guest—hesitant, pale, and carrying more dread than daylight.

The blizzard still hurled itself against the windows in icy fists, but inside the inn a different storm gathered: quiet, invisible, thick with unsaid truths. Too many secrets pressed against too many fragile walls.

Clara felt that pressure the moment her feet touched the kitchen floor.

She moved automatically—retrieving mugs, straightening trays, brushing flour from the counter—but her mind churned like the snow caught in the wind.

You are next to forget.

The note slipped beneath the door to Esther's office door hours earlier still sat like a burning coal behind her ribs.

Someone inside the inn wasn't just threatening them.

They were escalating.

And Clara intended to stop them.

She tightened her ponytail, breathed deeply, and anchored herself to her purpose:

Find the truth.

Protect Amelia.

Follow every clue.

And right now, that meant Doris Finch.

Doris stood at the kitchen island, folding napkins with trembling fingers. She'd insisted on keeping busy, but Clara knew the difference between helpful distraction and fear running wild.

The napkins were already folded. Twice.

Clara approached gently. "Doris? We need to talk."

Doris froze mid-fold, shoulders curling inward. "I suppose we do."

Clara guided her to the small table near the pantry. Doris sank into the chair as though her robe weighed fifty pounds. Lady Grey hopped onto the adjacent stool, fixing her with an unblinking stare—the feline equivalent of *We're listening*.

Clara sat opposite. "Doris... last night you said Covington recognized your name. And that you argued."

Doris's hands fluttered into her lap. "Argued, yes. But I didn't kill him." Her voice cracked—part defensive, part desperate. "I'm not capable of something like that."

"I'm not accusing you," Clara said softly. "But I need the truth. All of it. Someone stole the ornaments. Someone left that note for Amelia. And someone is playing a very dangerous game with all of us."

Doris swallowed hard.

Then whispered, "He was blackmailing me."

Clara didn't flinch. "Over Paul's art dealings?"

Doris's voice broke. "Yes."

She twisted the napkin until its corners frayed. "Years ago... before Paul died... he got caught up in a forgery ring. He didn't know at first. But by the time he realized what he was involved in, it was too late. Covington exposed everything. He wasn't malicious. But Paul never recovered from the shame."

Clara steadied her breath. "I'm sorry, Doris."

Doris nodded, eyes shining. "I thought it was over. Then last month Covington wrote to me. Demanded cash. Said he'd found new evidence—something that proved Paul's involvement went deeper than he'd ever admitted."

"Extortion," Clara murmured.

"I didn't want anyone to know," Doris said, wiping at her cheeks. "But I paid him once. Just once. I hoped he'd leave me alone. But when he came here this weekend..." Her voice shook. "He wanted more."

Clara fought down a flare of anger—not at Doris, but at the cruelty of Covington's desperation. "And you argued."

"Yes. But after that, I went straight to the kitchen. I stayed until the lights went out. I didn't hurt him." Her voice trembled. "I swear I didn't."

Clara believed her. Doris could be flustered, dramatic, meddlesome—but she wasn't a killer.

"Why didn't you tell Amelia?" Clara asked quietly.

"Because she already carries too much." Doris wrung the napkin until it trembled. "And because Covington said something that scared me. That he'd found something connected to the Monarch Society. Something hidden here in the inn."

Clara's heart dipped. "And someone was following him."

Doris nodded, her voice barely a breath. "He said they didn't want him talking."

A cold draft swept through the kitchen, raising goosebumps along Clara's arms.

"Thank you," Clara said. "I know that wasn't easy."

Doris nodded shakily. "Just... please don't think I—"

"I don't," Clara assured her. "But stay with the others. No wandering alone."

When Doris left, Clara stood for a long moment, breathing

through the tangle in her mind.

The sleigh in the pantry.

The missing ornaments.

The secret drawer in Esther's desk.

The crown ornament.

And now—Covington being hunted.

Answers had to be somewhere.

She crossed to the pantry—the place where secrets seemed to gather like dust. She reached for the shallow drawer beneath the counter, the one usually filled with ribbon ties and spare tags.

When she opened it, something thin slid forward.

Not a tag.

Not a recipe card.

A ledger.

Covington's ledger.

Clara lifted it with trembling hands.

The leather was worn, the pages fragile—yet the handwriting inside was unmistakable. She flipped through entry after entry, pulse hammering.

All cash.

All questionable.

All connected to valuable ornaments.

"Appraisal fee – $900 – cash"

"Verification – Murano teardrop – $1200 – cash"

"Assessment – Bavarian sphere – $700 – cash"

"Recollection consultation – $1500 – cash"

Bribes?

Payoffs?

Under-the-table deals?

Lady Grey hopped onto the counter, sniffing the ledger with a low, uneasy trill as Clara turned another page.

Scribbled notes filled the margins:

"Crown ornament – find. Before they do."

"Truth buried at T.B. Inn."

"Monarch debt must not be paid."

Clara's breath hitched. "Oh no..."

Covington hadn't come for a holiday festival.

He'd come chasing the crown ornament—the same one Esther insisted must stay hidden.

And someone else had come chasing **him.**

She flipped to the last page.

There, underlined twice in jagged strokes:

"Pike is lying."

Clara's stomach dropped.

Alden Pike—whose suitcase Lady Grey exposed.

Whose forged deeds she'd seen.

Whose impatience masked something gnawing beneath.

This snowstorm wasn't trapping them by chance.

It was trapping them **with him.**

"Clara?"

Mr. Lark stood in the doorway, face pale and drawn tight.

She showed him the ledger.

He skimmed it, and the color drained further. "Clara... this isn't simply criminal. This is historical. Generational. These ornaments—" he tapped the page "—carried Monarch bargains. Hidden agreements. If Covington rediscovered the crown—"

"He was killed for it," Clara whispered.

Lady Grey's tail puffed sharply.

"Hiding the truth was the Monarchs' entire foundation," Mr. Lark said grimly. "And some foundations crumble violently when disturbed."

Before Clara could respond, Lady Grey's head snapped toward the hallway.

Then—

CRASH.

A sharp explosion of breaking glass shattered the inn's fragile calm.

Clara sprinted into the hall.

Something round and glinting rolled across the wooden floor, leaving a faint ribbon of color in its wake.

An ornament.

Shattered pieces glittered near the baseboard like ruby shards scattered across the dim corridor.

Clara crouched, breath catching.

Inside one broken fragment—etched faintly but unmistakably— was the Monarch butterfly emblem.

A warning.

A threat.

A declaration.

Lady Grey growled low, golden eyes narrowed to slits.

Clara slowly lifted her gaze—

Just in time to see a shadow slip around the far corner of the hall.

Someone had been standing there.

Watching her.

Listening.

And running the moment she arrived.

Clara's fingers curled around the glass fragment.

Someone inside the inn wanted her to know:

They weren't done yet.

Not even close.

Chapter 13

Paws and Patterns

Lady Grey was becoming increasingly convinced of one thing:

Humans were terribly messy creatures.

They dropped things. They bumped into furniture. They shattered priceless ornaments with the same careless ease they misplaced socks.

Worst of all, they were utterly oblivious to trails of evidence lying directly beneath their noses.

Good thing the inn had her.

She padded toward the glittering shards scattered across the upstairs hallway—each falling star of glass catching the lantern light in a frosted shimmer. Clara lingered at the top of the stairs behind her, breath unsteady, but Lady Grey did not wait for permission.

This was her territory.

Her investigation.

She moved with deliberate grace, paws threading between the shards with a precision no human could ever hope to match. She lowered her nose and inhaled.

The ornament smelled of varnish and age—memories trapped

under layers of dust. But beneath those familiar notes, Lady Grey detected something else.

Ink.

Old parchment.

And a faint metallic tang that did not belong to any Farnsworth heirloom.

Her whiskers twitched.

She crouched, examining the largest remaining piece—a winter-berry curve of crimson glass. Something pale peeked from beneath it.

Lady Grey nudged the shard aside with her paw.

It tipped smoothly.

Beneath it lay a tightly rolled piece of parchment, no bigger than a matchstick.

Well, well, well.

She sniffed it. No peppermint. No cologne. Only ink. Dust. Secrets.

Lady Grey took it delicately between her teeth. Parchment tasted like stale crackers dipped in library glue, but she was willing to make sacrifices for her humans.

Behind her, Clara gasped. "Lady Grey? What is that?"

Grey did not respond. Humans always questioned the process before the work was finished.

She padded toward the stairs—

—when a cold draft slid across her fur, raising every hair along her spine in electric warning.

Someone was coming.

Lady Grey froze, ears swiveling toward the far end of the hall. Footsteps—slow, heavy—echoed against the wooden walls. With them came shifting scents:

Cedar polish.

Sweet pipe tobacco.

And beneath it all—thin, trembling—fear.

No one downstairs smelled like that.

Grey darted beneath the old mahogany buffet table along the

hallway wall—a hulking furniture beast with enough shadow for three cats, though she would never dream of sharing.

She flattened herself against the baseboard.

Still.

Silent.

Invisible.

The footsteps stopped.

Inches away.

Only the low hum of the heater vent filled the quiet.

Then—a voice.

Low. Male. Familiar.

But muffled by wood and distance.

Lady Grey's spine tingled.

The figure crouched, breath steady—too steady. The kind of steadiness that came only when someone was extremely nervous.

The scent hit her fully now: cedar, tobacco... and guilt.

Then came the whisper—soft as snow sliding down a roof:

"The map can't be found."

Lady Grey's pupils dilated.

The boots pivoted sharply. Footsteps retreated—faster this time, as if a decision had been made in a single, fearful heartbeat.

The map must not be found.

Interesting.

And Grey held something in her mouth that someone very much wanted hidden.

She waited until the last echo faded before slipping from beneath the buffet. Scroll still clutched delicately, she padded toward the stairs.

Clara rushed forward, face pale. "Lady Grey! What did you—oh."

Her eyes widened at the tiny scroll dangling from Grey's mouth.

Dropping to her knees, Clara held out her hand. "What did you find, sweetheart?"

Lady Grey placed the parchment into her palm with regal ceremony.

Clara unrolled it with trembling fingers.

Her breath stilled. "Covington's handwriting. And... this looks like an inventory list." She scanned further. "Notes about each ornament. Hidden markings. Dates. Transactions. He hid this inside the ornament. He must've known someone was after his research."

Lady Grey purred softly, tail curling in satisfied poise.

Yes. She *was* exceptional. Finally someone noticed.

Clara swallowed, still reading. "Someone broke this ornament because they were looking for this." Her voice dropped to a tense whisper. "If Covington hid papers inside ornaments... what else did he hide?"

Before Lady Grey could encourage further revelations, a faint creak drifted up from downstairs.

Both of them stilled.

Another sound followed—soft, like a door shifting quietly in its frame.

Lady Grey's tail flicked sharply.

Someone else was awake.

Clara rose slowly. "Grey... whatever you just uncovered—it's bigger than an inventory list."

Lady Grey stepped closer, a low rumble vibrating beneath her ribs.

Because drifting from the shadows below came a voice—barely audible, but unmistakably the same one from the hallway:

"It can't be found. It must not be found."

Clara's breath hitched.

Lady Grey pressed against her ankle, guiding her toward the stairs with purposeful, determined steps.

The storm clawed at the windows. The inn's walls groaned under the weight of wind and history.

And somewhere below them, a secret breathed in the dark.

The whisper came again—clearer now, certain:

"The map can't be found."
And Lady Grey knew:
Whatever lay hidden inside the ornaments...
whatever Covington uncovered...
whatever "map" someone feared being discovered...
...was now squarely in her paws.

Chapter 14

A Family Secret

Amelia had read the words on the parchment three times now, and each pass made her pulse throb harder—heavier —until it felt as though her own heartbeat were echoing through the ink.

Farnsworth Collection — Verified Items (see crown notation)

Farnsworth Collection — Missing Items (suspected hidden)

T.B. Inn Registry — Quiet ledger

Farnsworth Collection.

Her name.

Her family.

Her grandmother.

Not just the warm, clever woman who taught her to braid garlands and bake gingerbread.

Not just the patient innkeeper woven into Tumblebrook's fabric.

But something else entirely.

A keeper of Monarch Society artifacts.

A guardian of secrets.

Amelia sank into the nearest wingback chair. The fire crackled low beside her, the storm hurling sheets of snow against the windows with restless fury. Clara hovered close, trembling slightly as she reread the inventory list Lady Grey had uncovered. Mr. Lark paced in slow, tight circles, hands clasped behind his back like a nervous professor circling a test he wished he hadn't assigned.

"This is... extraordinary," he murmured, voice thin with awe and fear. "And deeply troubling."

Clara nodded. "Covington wasn't just cataloging antiques. He was tracking Monarch artifacts—coded pieces, missing items. And this... this Farnsworth Collection? That's personal."

Amelia exhaled shakily. "Grandma always said the inn had history. Secret corners. Stories waiting for the right snowfall." Her throat constricted. "I didn't think she meant *this*."

Lady Grey hopped onto Amelia's lap, settling into a warm, purring loaf, as though she sensed Amelia needed grounding more than explanations.

Mr. Lark finally paused his pacing. Behind the lenses of his glasses, his eyes softened—an expression Amelia had rarely seen on him. "Esther Farnsworth was many things. Private. Perceptive. Protective. If she hid Monarch artifacts..." His voice dipped. "It was not done lightly."

Clara lowered herself into the chair opposite her. "Amelia—we need answers. Real ones. Not folklore."

Amelia nodded.

And she knew exactly who might have them.

Uncle Frank.

Esther's last surviving son.

The family's reluctant historian.

If anyone knew the truth, he did.

She rose abruptly. "I'm calling him."

Clara blinked. "Now? In this storm?"

"Now," Amelia repeated, pulse tightening. "Before this gets worse."

Reception during winter storms was always unreliable at the inn, but tonight it was worse—one trembling bar blinking like a nervous firefly.

Amelia stood near the kitchen window, the only spot where a stubborn signal sometimes slipped through. Lady Grey trotted after her, tail held high like a tiny banner of determination.

"Come on," Amelia whispered. "Just one call. Please."

She dialed.

One ring.

Two.

Three.

Static crackled. Then—

"Amelia?" a faint voice rasped.

Relief flooded her. "Uncle Frank! I'm sorry to call so late, but it's urgent."

"Storm's bad," he croaked. "Barely hearin' ya."

"I know. Just—listen. We found something at the inn. Something about Grandma. About the Monarch Society."

Silence.

Then—a clatter, as though something had dropped on his end.

"Amelia," Frank whispered, sharp and hoarse, "whatever you found... put it back."

Her stomach dropped. "What?"

"Don't dig," he hissed. "Not in the Farnsworth things. Not in the old drawers."

"We already opened the drawer," Amelia said. "We found letters. A note about a crown ornament—"

Static surged violently, buzzing like hornets.

"Amelia—stop. Stop now."

"Uncle Frank, please," she whispered. "I need to know what she was protecting. Why our family is tied to this... collection."

A long breath crackled over the line.

And when he spoke again, decades of weight seeped through each syllable.

"Your grandmother didn't just work the Monarch galas," he said. "She safeguarded their artifacts. Especially during Prohibition."

Amelia froze. "Artifacts? Why her?"

"'Cause Esther Farnsworth was trusted—by everyone. The Monarchs. Their rivals. Folks needed places to stash things—gold, ledgers, deals. The inn was neutral ground."

Amelia stared toward the parlor, mind racing. "So the inn... it wasn't just a place for holiday tourism."

"No," Frank said. "It was a front. A meeting ground. A safe house. And a storage site, back when Tumblebrook was dyin' on its feet."

Clara and Mr. Lark exchanged stunned, breathless looks.

"Artifacts," Amelia echoed. "What exactly were they?"

"Ornaments," Frank said grimly. "But not the decorative kind. They were records. Ledgers disguised in glass and silver. Promises carved into metal. The crown ornament was the worst of 'em."

"Why dangerous?"

"Because it held names," Frank said. "The Monarch leaders. Their alliances. Their betrayals. Who owed what. Who broke their oaths." His voice dropped to a ragged whisper. "If that ornament resurfaces... so will the Society."

A cold shiver slipped down Amelia's spine.

"You're telling me the Monarch Society still exists."

"It never ended," Frank breathed. "It just... went quiet. But artifacts wake old blood. And older grudges."

Amelia swallowed hard. "Frank... did Grandma hide the crown ornament here?"

Static swallowed his answer.

"Uncle Frank!" she cried.

The line stumbled back—faint, frantic. "She hid more than ornaments, Amelia. More than the crown. You're not safe. The people who want those artifacts—"

The call snapped.

Silence crashed into the room.

Amelia lowered the phone slowly, pulse hammering.

Clara stepped forward. "What did he say?"

Amelia sank onto the arm of a chair, fingers trembling. "Everything. And not nearly enough."

She recounted the conversation.

Clara went pale. Mr. Lark looked stricken.

"So the ornaments held blackmail," Clara whispered. "Real power."

"And Esther hid them," Mr. Lark said, voice thin. "Right here."

Amelia exhaled shakily. Lady Grey bumped her leg, purring—a steady vibration amid chaos.

"We have to keep searching," Amelia said quietly. "If Grandma hid something... Covington was close to finding it."

"Close enough to die for it," Clara murmured.

Mr. Lark straightened. "If the ornaments contain Monarch secrets, the inn is the most logical hiding place. Esther understood concealment. Intimately."

Amelia nodded. "Then we search. Carefully."

Clara retrieved a lantern, its glow pooling warm amber across the parlor. Together, the three of them moved slowly—checking moldings, hearth edges, and old floorboards that had held generations of Farnsworth gatherings.

Lady Grey trotted ahead, tail flicking with focused importance.

"Careful," Clara murmured. "Some of these boards are older than we are."

Mr. Lark knelt by the hearth, fingers brushing seams in the floor. "Esther was a master of hiding things in plain sight."

Amelia drifted toward the place where the candle had toppled earlier. If the hidden envelope had been tucked there...

What else might have been waiting?

Lady Grey abruptly stopped in the center of the room.

Tap.

Tap-tap.

Amelia spun. "What is it, girl?"

Lady Grey tapped the floorboard again.

It moved.

Barely—but undeniably.

Amelia dropped to her knees. Clara raised the lantern higher, casting golden light across the wood.

Mr. Lark inhaled sharply. "Is that...?"

"Yes," Amelia whispered. "A seam."

A hidden one—so fine it vanished unless seen from the perfect angle...

or discovered by a cat with impeccable instincts.

Amelia pressed the board.

It lifted—just a fraction.

Her pulse quickened.

Clara crouched beside her. "Do we... open it?"

Amelia hesitated.

Her grandmother's voice whispered across years: *Some things stay buried for a reason.*

But a man was dead.

The ornaments were stolen.

Someone was leaving threats.

And the past wasn't waiting for her permission.

"Yes," she whispered. "We open it."

Together, she and Clara slid their fingers beneath the edge and lifted.

The old wood groaned.

A concealed hatch revealed itself—dark, narrow, waiting beneath the parlor floor.

Amelia stared into the shadowed space, heart pounding.

Whatever Esther Farnsworth hid there...

...was about to change everything.

Chapter 15

The Hidden Cellar

The hatch yawned open like a dark wooden mouth in the center of the parlor floor, exhaling a breath of stale, trapped air that skimmed across Clara's cheeks. She shivered—not from cold, but from the prickling certainty that whatever lay beneath the boards had been waiting for decades.

Waiting for *this* moment.

Waiting for *them*.

Amelia knelt beside her, lantern trembling faintly in her grip. Lady Grey perched on her shoulder—rare, regal, perfectly balanced —her golden eyes fixed unblinkingly on the darkness below.

Clara drew in a steady breath. "All right," she whispered. "Let's see what your grandmother was hiding."

A single wooden ladder led down into the void, its rungs pale with dust and bowed with age. The space below swallowed the lantern light, revealing only the faint outline of stone.

Clara gripped the ladder. "I'll go first."

Amelia grabbed her sleeve. "Be careful."

Lady Grey offered a pointed, reproachful *mrrp* before Clara could reply.

"I know," Clara sighed. "Today, I promise."

She began her descent.

With every rung, the cold deepened—carrying dust, earth, and the sharp tang of metal. By the time her boots reached solid stone, her breath puffed visibly in the lantern glow.

"Okay," she called up. "I'm down. But this ladder feels older than Mr. Lark's folklore collection."

Amelia descended after her. Lady Grey leapt from her shoulder and landed beside Clara as gracefully as falling snow.

Amelia's boots touched stone and she breathed, "Oh... wow."

The lantern's light expanded across the space.

A forgotten wine cellar stretched before them—stone walls damp with age, the granite floor fractured from decades of settling. Shelves that once held bottles now sagged under the weight of wooden crates.

Dusty wooden crates with curling, faded labels:

M.S. – Winter Claims

F.S. – Private Stock

Glass: Handle Carefully

Payment, 1929

Clara's breath hitched. "This place is enormous."

"Not enormous," Amelia murmured. "Hidden."

They moved deeper inside, lantern swinging, shadows stretching long across the walls. Some crates sat open, their lids splintered. Others remained sealed with fraying rope. In one corner, a long table slumped beneath a dusty sheet.

Clara approached the nearest open crate and lifted the lantern.

Her stomach tightened.

Inside lay shattered ornaments—glass shards in ruby, sapphire, emerald. Some pieces still bore etched markings that matched the inventory list hidden in Covington's ornament.

Not accidents.

Not age.

Deliberately smashed.

Amelia knelt beside her. "Why would Grandma destroy them?"

"She didn't," Clara said quietly. "These breaks are newer. See? No yellowing. No dust in the fractures." She swallowed. "Someone else did this."

Lady Grey hissed faintly, ears flattening as she sniffed the air.

Clara crossed to the next crate. Metal ornaments this time—silver bells, snowflakes, miniature figurines—each engraved with intricate patterns. She lifted one.

A Monarch butterfly. Sharp, unmistakable.

"Amelia..." Clara breathed. "This whole crate is Monarch-coded ornaments."

Amelia's eyes glistened. "She kept them. Even after everything fell apart."

Clara set the ornament down carefully.

They turned toward the table. Clara lifted the sheet.

Relics waited beneath:

Stacks of parchment.

Sealed envelopes.

A ledger branded with a Monarch butterfly deep in its leather cover.

A wooden box locked with a heavy clasp.

Amelia touched the ledger with reverent fingers. "An original Monarch ledger."

Clara opened it gently. The yellowed pages revealed:

Transactions — Winter Gala 1924

Acquisitions — Private Orders

Sealed Agreements — Restricted Access

Farnsworth — Custodial Record

Clara exhaled. "Your grandmother wasn't just protecting artifacts... she was protecting *evidence*. Everything they did in secret."

"And she carried it alone," Amelia whispered. "For decades."

Lady Grey nudged her ankle, purring softly—a silent pledge of solidarity.

Clara's gaze caught on a sealed envelope resting on the table, set slightly apart.

To My Heir

Amelia froze.

Clara raised the lantern. "I think it's time."

Amelia lifted the envelope with both hands, holding it as if it were something fragile and beloved. She broke the seal.

Clara steadied the lantern while Amelia unfolded the soft, worn paper.

Esther Farnsworth's elegant handwriting filled the page.

Amelia read aloud:

My Dearest Heir,

If you are reading this, then the ornaments have returned to the inn and danger has returned with them. The Monarch Society believed its legacy to be power and prestige. They were wrong. Their influence was built on deception and greed.

I hid the artifacts entrusted to me not to protect the Society, but to protect the town from what those artifacts contained. Within these crates lie the remains of their secrets—shattered where I could shatter them, concealed where breaking them would unleash old debts.

Three members used the ornaments to defraud. Three used them to blackmail. One used them to silence.

I could not expose them without risking retaliation. But you may live in a safer time. If the Society stirs again, you must decide whether to reveal the truth, or bury it once more.

The crown ornament holds the key. It must never fall into the wrong hands.

Protect the inn. Protect our legacy. Protect Tumblebrook.

With love and caution,

E.F.

Amelia sat back heavily against a crate, the letter trembling in her grip.

Clara knelt beside her. "She wasn't hiding things *for* the Monarch Society... she was hiding things *from* them."

Amelia shut her eyes. "She bore this alone."

"And you're not doing that," Clara said gently. "We're with you. All the way."

Lady Grey jumped into Amelia's lap and pressed her forehead to Amelia's chin—quiet feline comfort, steady and warm.

Amelia drew a slow breath. "We need to take the letters upstairs. The ledger. The inventory. Everything. Then we need a plan."

Clara nodded. "And we should hide anything we don't carry. Whoever smashed that ornament might still be searching."

A faint chill swept through the cellar.

Clara stiffened. "Did you feel that?"

Amelia straightened. "Draft?"

"No," Clara whispered. "Not a draft."

Lady Grey's ears shot forward. Her head whipped toward the ladder.

Clara followed her gaze.

Above them, the lantern flame flickered violently.

A soft creak echoed across the parlor floor.

Not the storm.

Not the house settling.

Someone standing directly above the open hatch.

Listening.

Watching.

Clara raised the lantern, but before the glow reached the ladder, the flame sputtered—

—and snapped out.

Darkness swallowed them whole.

Then—

Footsteps.

Retreating quickly.

Light enough for stealth.

Urgent enough for fear.

Amelia grabbed Clara's hand. Lady Grey pressed tight against Clara's boot, tense and alert.

The footsteps raced across the parlor floor...

...and vanished into the storm-lit shadows.

Someone had seen them open the hatch.

Someone knew what they had found.

And they were already running to stop them from uncovering more.

Chapter 16

Cat Among Shadows

Lady Grey emerged from the cellar hatch like a tiny, furious guardian goddess.

Her tail had puffed to nearly double its size—an indignant feather duster of outrage—as she glared at the open hatch behind her. No one else seemed properly alarmed.

Humans.

They climbed out one by one—Amelia first, pale and shaken; then Clara, gripping the lantern; then Mr. Lark, wide-eyed behind quivering spectacles. The air above the hatch still hummed with the fading echo of retreating footsteps, but only Lady Grey seemed aware of how close danger had come.

She planted herself in front of the opening with all the dignity a seven-pound cat could summon.

This was her post.

Her inn.

Her humans.

Her mystery.

If someone wanted to sneak in, they would have to go through her.

And she was not in a sharing mood.

Amelia knelt, reaching to stroke her, but Lady Grey stepped back. Not now. Not until she knew her people were safe.

Clara whispered, breath tight, "Someone was definitely listening."

Lady Grey flicked her tail in crisp, unimpressed agreement.

Mr. Lark cleared his throat. "We should conceal the hatch again. Whoever was up here—"

Lady Grey's ears snapped upright.

A whisper.

Faint.

Threadlike.

Floating along the old hallway's draft.

"Amelia..."

Lady Grey pivoted instantly toward the stairs.

No hesitation.

No fear.

Pure instinct.

She bolted.

"Lady Grey!" Amelia called.

But the cat was already gone.

The voice drifted from above—warped, carried by the storm's moan.

"Amelia... Am-li-aaa..."

Not playful.

Not kind.

Not familiar.

A predator's whisper.

Lady Grey slunk up the stairs, low to the carpet, whiskers trembling as she scanned the landing. Frost crusted the windowpanes, and the hush of snow smothered every sound. Shadows hunched in corners like nervous guests.

There—again.

"Amelia..."

Closer.

Left.

Lady Grey quickened her pace. A cold draft brushed her whiskers, pulling her toward the guest corridor—the same path the booted intruder had taken hours earlier.

The far door eased shut with a soft, deliberate *click*.

Lady Grey froze.

Listened.

Waited.

Silence.

Then, drifting from beneath the door, came a scent that curled her lip:

Burnt sugar.

Bitter spice.

And below it—something chemical. Artificial.

A scent trying too hard to hide itself.

Lady Grey's ears twitched.

She turned toward the kitchen.

Into the Kitchen

The kitchen door stood open by an inch. Lady Grey pressed her nose into the gap and slipped through.

A soft clatter echoed from the far counter. She crouched behind the butcher-block table, ears swiveling like tiny satellite dishes.

The stove's pilot flame cast a dim flicker across pans and tiles. Shadows stretched long and breathless along the walls.

Lady Grey sniffed.

Once.

Twice.

There—on the floor.

Crumbs.

Not just any crumbs—Clara's gingerbread crumbs, rich with cinnamon, molasses, and pride. Lady Grey recognized that scent anywhere.

And more importantly:

Clara never left crumbs.

Ever.

Lady Grey followed the trail, step by deliberate step. It led her past the cooling racks, past the spice cabinet, to the far counter.

She hopped up with a silent, practiced spring.

A single teacup sat waiting.

Not one of the everyday mugs—one of Amelia's specialty cocoa service cups, heavy porcelain meant to impress.

Lady Grey sniffed the rim.

Bitter.

Sharp.

Wrong.

Cocoa should smell like warm hugs and winter comfort.

This smelled like danger pretending to be sweetness.

Her fur bristled.

Someone had tampered with a drink.

Someone had intended harm.

Lady Grey narrowed her eyes. Humans rarely responded to subtle warnings.

Chaos then.

Her specialty.

She shifted her stance beside the cup. Lifted a paw. Paused—just long enough for dramatic effect.

Then—

WHACK.

The teacup flipped sideways, shattering across the tile in an eruption of porcelain shards. A pale powder fanned out with the cocoa— gritty, foreign, unmistakably wrong.

Not cocoa.

Not sugar.

Not spices.

Poison.

Lady Grey hissed loudly—the feline equivalent of ringing a brass alarm bell.

Footsteps hammered down the hallway.

"What was that?" Clara called.

"Kitchen!" Amelia's voice followed.

Lady Grey sat proudly beside the broken cup, tail curled like a victorious punctuation mark.

Clara arrived first and gasped. "Oh no. No—no, no..."

Amelia skidded in behind her. "What—Lady Grey, what did you...?"

Clara crouched. "She didn't break this by accident." She lifted a shard, her voice tight. "She wants us to *see* this."

Amelia stared at the powder. Color drained from her cheeks. "Clara... that's not cocoa mix."

Mr. Lark rushed in and stopped short. "Is that...?"

Clara dipped a clean spoon into the residue, sniffed, and recoiled. "Not cocoa. Definitely not."

Lady Grey flicked her tail. Exactly.

"Was this meant for one of us?" Amelia whispered.

Clara's jaw tightened. "No. I think it was meant for *you*."

Lady Grey pushed her head firmly against Amelia's ankle, urging her backward.

Danger had entered the kitchen.

Danger that smelled of cedar and tobacco.

Danger that whispered Amelia's name in empty halls.

Lady Grey would not tolerate it.

Amelia steadied her breath. "We need everyone together. We need to figure out who—"

Lady Grey froze.

Her gaze lifted to the copper pot hanging above the stove. The polished metal reflected the dim light like a warped mirror.

Movement.

Behind her.

Silent.

Shifting.

Lady Grey's pupils widened.

In the pot's curved reflection stood the silhouette of a tall figure in the doorway.

Watching them.

Watching Amelia.

Lady Grey spun around—

Nothing.

The doorway was empty.

But the faint scent of cedar and pipe tobacco clung to the air like a ghostly fingerprint.

Lady Grey curled her lip.

The hunter had been here.

Close enough to touch.

Close enough to strike.

And now they had vanished again—slipping through the inn's shadows like smoke.

Lady Grey stared at the copper pot's reflection as the last trace of the silhouette dissolved into the dim.

Someone had been there.

And they would be back.

Chapter 17

Snowstorm Suspicions

The parlor *should* have felt warm.

A fire crackled in the hearth. Garlands framed the doorway. Snowflakes tapped the windows like tiny, impatient guests. Lantern light glowed through cinnamon-sweet air.

But none of that warmth reached Amelia.

Not with six unsettled townspeople gathered before her—pacing, whispering, glowering—as if the inn itself had transformed into a simmering pressure cooker.

And all because someone had tried to poison her.

Cold dread still clung under her ribs, heavy and bruising.

Clara hovered at her elbow like an anxious general. Lady Grey perched atop the sofa with her tail wrapped tightly around her paws, golden eyes tracking every movement as though conducting her own feline interrogation.

Amelia swallowed and stepped forward.

"Everyone," she said, "we need to talk."

Alden Pike—naturally—responded first. His bark of incredulous laughter echoed off the garlands. "Talk? What we need is to *leave!*

You're the one keeping us here, Amelia. This storm is bad enough without—"

"You saw the bridge," Clara snapped. "It's underwater and half collapsed. No one's going anywhere unless they can sprout wings."

"I could get across if someone would give me a ride into town—"

"Through a blizzard?" Clara scoffed. "Great. Bring a parachute."

Doris wrung her trembling hands, wilted beside the Christmas tree. "This is awful... I can't stand all this arguing. Someone's going to get hurt."

"Someone *already* got hurt," Pike shot back, jabbing a finger at Amelia. "Someone tried to poison her cocoa, and you want us to sit around and—"

"Mr. Pike." Amelia's voice cut cleanly through the chaos—calmer than she felt. "Sit down."

Miraculously, he did. Grumbling, but he sat.

Ezra lingered near the window, hunched and tight, like a startled bird. The storm howled behind him, wind whistling around the frame in mournful moans.

Mr. Lark hovered near the mantle, gaze downcast, fingers worrying the corner of a leather-bound book.

Amelia steadied her breath.

"You all know something is happening," she said. "Covington's death wasn't an accident. The ornaments keep vanishing. Someone is leaving threatening notes. And now—" her voice faltered, "—someone tampered with cocoa meant for me."

Gasps rippled through the room. Doris clapped both hands to her mouth.

Pike surged to his feet. "I say Lark did it."

Mr. Lark jolted, eyes wide. "Excuse me?"

"You were the last one near the kitchen," Pike barked. "You and Covington were practically twins when it came to antique nonsense. You know everything about those cursed ornaments. Seems exactly like the kind of man who'd kill to protect them."

Mr. Lark flushed a furious crimson—not guilt, but insult.

"Edward and I were colleagues. Shared academic interests. That does *not* make me a murderer."

"Oh, please," Pike sneered. "You skulk around Gossamer Fables muttering about Monarch secrets. You're obsessed with the past."

Clara stepped in. "Accusing everyone at random does nothing but stir panic—"

"Oh, you'd know all about stirring panic," Pike snapped. "Convenient how Lady Grey 'discovers' things whenever *you're* nearby. How do we know you're not planting clues?"

Clara stared at him. "Are you seriously accusing a *cat?*"

Lady Grey's tail twitched—slow and lethal.

Doris swayed. "Please... stop shouting... I can't..."

Her knees buckled.

Amelia lunged, catching her just in time. "Doris!"

Clara slid a pillow under her head. "Easy. Breathe."

"She fainted again," Ezra murmured from his corner.

Amelia dabbed Doris's forehead. "You're all right. You're safe."

"Nothing is safe," Doris whispered. "Someone in this room... wants us scared."

Clara's gaze darted toward Ezra. "You okay?"

He nodded too quickly. "Fine. Just... don't like crowds." His eyes flicked toward the parlor door.

"Ezra," Amelia said gently, "we need everyone together."

"I need air," he whispered.

Before anyone could stop him, he slipped out.

Pike groaned. "Perfect. People wandering off. This is how horror movies start."

"This is *not* a horror movie," Amelia said tightly. "This is Tumblebrook. My home. And I won't let anything happen to any of you."

"Too late," Pike muttered.

Clara leaned close, voice low. "He's right about one thing—Ezra shouldn't be alone."

"I know," Amelia murmured. "But chasing him will only make things worse."

The storm battered harder against the windows. Garlands trembled. Lady Grey paced along the sofa back, tail flicking in agitation.

Amelia scanned the room:

Pike—furious, paranoid, hiding more than he admitted.

Mr. Lark—distressed, weighed down by knowledge he wasn't sharing.

Doris—terrified and unraveling.

Ezra—skittish, secretive, and now missing.

Clara—steadfast and exhausted.

Lady Grey—tense, alert, ready.

Every person in this inn had a reason to fear the truth.

And that frightened Amelia more than the poison.

"Listen," she said, voice firmer, "the storm may be trapping us here, but we cannot turn on each other. That is exactly what the real culprit wants."

Pike rolled his eyes.

Mr. Lark pinched the bridge of his nose.

Doris whimpered softly.

"We stay together," Amelia continued. "No one wanders off. No one is alone. When Sheriff Daniels arrives tomorrow, he can take over. Until then—"

She stopped.

Above them—beyond beams and garlands—

A sound drifted down.

Soft.

Muffled.

Terrified.

A scream.

Clara's head snapped upward. Mr. Lark's book slipped from his trembling hands.

Pike paled. "What...what was that?"

The scream came again—higher, sharper, unmistakably panicked.

From the attic.

Lady Grey exploded off the sofa, streaking toward the stairs like a bolt of silver lightning.

"Someone's up there," Clara whispered.

Amelia's pulse crashed in her ears. "The attic."

Silence clamped down on the room like a lid.

Then—

A third scream erupted.

Desperate.

Human.

The attic waited.

And whatever was up there...

...was no longer hiding.

Chapter 18

The Missing Carver

Clara took the stairs two at a time.

The third scream had ripped through the inn like lightning—clean, vicious, and impossible to ignore—snapping every nerve taut and sending all of them bolting out of the parlor. Now her legs burned and her lungs ached, but she didn't slow.

Amelia was right beside her, pale and gripping the banister. Behind them, Pike puffed and muttered under his breath, and farther back Mr. Lark called for them to be careful.

Lady Grey streaked ahead—just a flash of silver and fierce certainty.

"Ezra," Clara gasped. It had to be Ezra. He'd vanished right after the argument, wound tight as a watch spring all evening. And that scream... there had been real terror in it.

At the top of the stairs, the hallway stretched like a narrow tunnel of shadows. Wind whistled along the eaves, making the old house creak as though it were remembering every winter it had ever endured.

Lady Grey sat rigid beside the door at the end of the hall—the attic stairwell. Her tail was puffed, pupils wide, ears pinned flat.

"There," Clara whispered. "She says it's there."

Amelia fumbled with the latch, hands trembling. "Ready?"

"No," Clara admitted. "But open it anyway."

The door groaned as it swung inward, exhaling a breath of cold air that skimmed across their faces. The attic steps rose in a steep, narrow climb, vanishing into darkness.

For one taut heartbeat, nobody moved.

Then Lady Grey darted up the stairs.

Clara followed.

Halfway up, the smell hit her—dust, old wood, paint, varnish... and beneath it, the faint metallic tang of fear.

"Ezra?" she called. "Ezra, can you hear me?"

A muffled sound answered. Not quite words. Not quite a groan. Something raw and in-between.

Clara's heart leapt. "He's up there!"

Amelia's lantern bobbed behind her, casting erratic, swinging shadows along the sloped ceiling as Clara reached the top and pushed into the attic.

Everything looked different in the wavering light.

Shadows clung to trunks and crates. Dust floated like pale ghosts. The small window at the back rattled under the storm's fists, the glass humming in its aging frame.

And there, lashed to a support beam—

"Clara," Amelia breathed, horror cracking her voice. "Oh my goodness."

Ezra was tied to a chair.

Rope bit into his wrists and ankles. A strip of fabric gagged his mouth. His head hung at an angle, eyes half-shut. One side of his face was red—he'd probably fought the gag.

For half a second, Clara's mind catalogued details—tight knots, scuffed boots, the tremor in his fingers.

Then the shock arrived.

"Ezra!"

She dropped to her knees, dust puffing up around her. "It's okay, we're here," she murmured, fumbling at the gag. "You're safe... just hold on."

He flinched, then blinked—slowly, painfully—focus returning in pieces.

Amelia set the lantern on a crate and flicked open the small knife she kept in her pocket, sawing through the rope at his wrists. Pike lingered at the attic entrance—not close enough to help, not far enough to deflect suspicion. Typical.

"Who did this?" Clara asked as she worked at the knot behind Ezra's head. "Ezra, can you hear me? Stay with us."

His skin was clammy, lips dry. When the gag finally came free, he sagged forward, wheezing.

"Water," he croaked.

"I'll get some." Amelia sprang toward the stairs. "Pike—stay with them."

"I'm not a nurse—"

"Then at least watch the doorway," Clara snapped. "If whoever did this comes back, I'd like a little warning."

Pike swallowed. "Right. Doorway. Sure. Fine." He shuffled to the top step, peering down like a reluctant sentry.

Lady Grey hopped onto a nearby trunk, fixing Ezra with a bright, unblinking stare. After a long, assessing moment, she sat—tail neatly curled—her approval cautious.

Clara softened her voice. "We're going to untie your legs, okay? You're safe."

Ezra managed a faint nod.

She cut the rope at his ankles. He winced as blood returned to his feet.

"Deep breaths," she coached gently. "Slow and steady."

Amelia reappeared moments later, cheeks flushed, a glass of water trembling in her hand. Ezra took it carefully, drinking in ragged, shallow sips.

"Thank you," he rasped.

Clara's pulse hammered. "Ezra, what happened? Who did this to you?"

He shut his eyes, as though gathering strength from the darkness behind them.

"They... didn't want me talking," he whispered. "About the ornaments."

Clara's breath stalled. "You mean Covington's work?"

"And yours," Amelia added. "He came to your cabin before the festival. You told us that much."

Ezra's gaze drifted toward the crates along the far wall, where old garlands and decorations slumped under faded sheets.

"The ornaments..." His voice was barely louder than the wind outside. "They're not what they seem."

Clara exchanged a glance with Amelia. "We're listening."

Ezra swallowed. "Covington came to me three weeks ago. Right before the snow started to stick. Said he'd found something big tied to the Monarch Society. Said he needed my hands."

"Your hands?" Clara repeated.

"For carving." His fingers twitched, calluses catching the lantern light. "He brought sketches. Photos. Measurements. Wanted replicas of certain ornaments. Exact replicas."

Clara's breath tightened. "He asked you to make duplicates."

Ezra nodded. "A silver sleigh. A crown. Two starbursts. A bell with a butterfly inside."

Air thinned around Clara.

Those weren't random pieces—they were the very ornaments entangled in the investigation: the sleigh from the pantry box, the crown in Esther's letter, the butterfly that kept resurfacing like a ghost.

"Why?" Amelia asked. "Did he tell you why he wanted duplicates?"

Ezra stared at the rattling window. "He said he was tired of being blamed. Said if the people who used those ornaments to hide their crimes wanted to keep their secrets locked away... he'd beat them at their own game."

Clara's voice turned thin. "He wanted to swap originals with fakes."

Ezra nodded. "Hide the real ones somewhere safe. Somewhere no one would think to look." His shoulders sagged. "He was scared, Clara. I've never seen a man so scared and still trying to swagger."

Whatever Covington had been—proud, prickly, tainted by scandal—he hadn't deserved to die beneath her tree.

"Did you finish the duplicates?" she asked softly.

"All but the crown," Ezra said. "He hadn't found it. Only descriptions. He was tracking it through letters, ledgers... your grandmother's things." He met Amelia's eyes. "He said the Farnsworth Collection was the last piece of the puzzle."

Amelia wrapped her arms around herself. "And when ornaments started disappearing..."

"You thought someone had taken the fakes," Clara finished. "That Covington had outsmarted them."

Ezra swallowed. "I hoped that meant the originals were safe." His voice roughened. "Then he died. And I knew someone had figured out what he was doing."

The attic seemed to shrink, the rafters pressing lower.

Pike crossed his arms. "This is exactly the sort of double-cross nonsense that gets people killed."

Clara ignored him. "Ezra, who else knew about the duplicates?"

"He wasn't telling anyone. Not even the people paying him. He didn't want anyone to know where the originals were going." He hesitated. "But when he left my cabin, he muttered something."

"What?"

"'The only place they never thought to look the first time.'"

Clara thought of the cellar hatch. The crates. Esther's careful hiding places.

"The hidden vault," she whispered.

Amelia nodded. "Grandma's wine cellar. If Covington found it..."

"...and someone else realized he had," Clara finished, "that gave them motive."

Ezra's hand drifted to the rope burn on his wrist. "If you hadn't come when you did..."

Lady Grey hopped down and sniffed Ezra's clothes—his trouser leg, his boots, his coat sleeve. Her tail flicked, undecided.

Clara noticed. Lady Grey trusted rarely—and never without reason.

"You need rest," Amelia said. "We'll get you downstairs by the fire."

"And then what?" Pike demanded. "Sing carols? We've got a tied-up carver, a dead man, a poison attempt, and someone wandering around swapping ornaments like playing cards."

"No one is pretending this is fine," Clara snapped. "But he can't answer anything if he collapses."

Before she could help Ezra stand, Lady Grey shifted.

The cat was suddenly, intensely interested in Ezra's coat pocket.

Clara watched her wedge her nose under the flap, then bat at it. Once. Twice. Again.

"What is it, girl?" Clara murmured.

Lady Grey ignored her, shoving deeper.

Ezra jerked. "Hey—careful—that's my—"

A slip of paper fluttered to the floor.

Lady Grey sat back, very pleased, flicking her tail toward it like she'd solved a riddle.

Clara unfolded it.

A receipt.

Hardware store. The next town over.

Her eyes scanned the lines.

Glass glue

Paint thinner (industrial strength)

Fine-grit sandpaper

Date: One week before the festival.

Clara's stomach lurched.

She looked up slowly.

Ezra had gone stone-still.

"Explain," she said quietly, "why you're buying supplies to repair —or alter—glass ornaments."

He said nothing.

Guilt flickered across his face, faint but unmistakable.

"The ornaments," he whispered, "they're not what they seem."

The little receipt crinkled in Clara's tightening hand.

She thought of the shattered ornaments in the cellar. The forged certificates. The duplicate sleigh. The Monarch ledger. The crown ornament everyone feared.

It would be so easy, wouldn't it?

To swap originals for fakes.

To "repair" glass just enough to erase the truth etched inside.

To make sure no one could ever read those secrets again.

"Ezra," she whispered, "what exactly have you been doing with those duplicates?"

He didn't answer.

Outside, the wind pummeled the roof, rattling the rafters.

Lady Grey's tail lashed—a grey metronome of warning.

And the slip of paper in Clara's palm felt heavier than any ornament.

Whatever Ezra had been before—a hermit, a witness, a victim—

One thing was suddenly, terribly clear:

Ezra the carver was no longer just tangled in the mystery.

He might be holding a chisel to the truth itself.

Chapter 19

The Cat's Witness

Lady Grey watched Ezra closely—closer than she'd watched anyone in a very long time.

Humans were endlessly chaotic creatures. They hid feelings behind cocoa mugs and knitted scarves, behind that peculiar habit of smiling when they were actually breaking apart. But Lady Grey didn't need any of that. She didn't need words.

She had senses sharper than any carving tool Ezra owned and instincts tuned tighter than a violin string.

Ezra, now wrapped in a blanket near the hearth, did not smell dangerous.

Not like the boots-man, who reeked of cedar polish, tobacco, and guilt.

Not like Pike, who smelled of metallic ink and self-inflicted desperation.

Not like Covington, whose coat had carried the damp scent of old fear the night he died beneath the Christmas tree.

Ezra smelled like varnish.

And sawdust.

And loneliness.

And regret—a scent Lady Grey knew well after a lifetime of knocking over Amelia's favorite vases.

So even as Clara asked her gentle questions, and Amelia hovered nearby like a snow-dusted guardian, and Mr. Lark wrung his hands until they resembled twisted bookmarks, Lady Grey curled herself beside Ezra's leg. Not touching, but close enough that he could feel her warmth if he needed it.

Even a human deserved that much.

Ezra noticed and blinked down at her. "You... trust me?"

Lady Grey blinked once.

Trust was far too strong a word.

But fear? True danger?

No. Ezra was not the enemy.

He patted her back with a shaking hand.

She tolerated it for a generous three seconds before slipping away when the room's energy shifted. Exhaustion replaced panic. Questions replaced shouting. The storm outside eased for a moment, and the tension inside thinned just enough for her to vanish into the shadows.

Her work was no longer in the parlor.

Her work lay elsewhere.

She flicked her tail and slipped out.

The inn was dim, lanterns guttering under the storm's relentless battering. Frost crawled along the windows like white vines. Every hallway felt deeper, darker, older.

Lady Grey moved silently across the floorboards.

But someone else moved, too.

Footsteps.

Soft.

Cautious.

Human.

She followed the scent first.

Alden Pike.

Ink.

Old receipts.

Stress.

And that sour musk of ambition curdled into greed.

He wasn't heading toward his room.

He was heading toward Amelia's office.

Toward locked drawers.

Toward paperwork.

Toward trouble.

Lady Grey narrowed her eyes.

She followed.

Into the Office

Pike closed the office door behind him—but not fully.

Humans rarely latched doors properly. A terrible habit. Extremely convenient for observant cats.

Lady Grey nudged the door open and slipped inside.

The room smelled of cedar shelves, aging paper, fresh ink, and Amelia's subtle lavender perfume. But tonight, something else threaded through it all.

Burning.

Pike crouched beside the tiny office fireplace, frantically feeding papers into the flames. His silhouette jerked and twitched in the firelight, throwing warped shadows across the walls.

Lady Grey froze behind a chair.

"Can't let them see... can't let them know..." Pike muttered, shoving another envelope into the fire. "They don't understand business. They don't know what it takes..."

He yanked open a locked drawer Amelia always kept secured—yet somehow, he had a key.

Or something sharp enough to stand in for one.

Lady Grey's tail puffed.

This was wrong.

This was dangerous.

She stepped forward.

Pike didn't notice. He was too busy ripping open envelopes and tossing documents into the flames.

Lady Grey hissed.

Pike whirled. "You!"

She flattened her ears. A perfectly clear response.

"You little menace," he snapped. "Why are you always under my feet?"

Lady Grey leapt onto the desk, landing as lightly as snowfall.

"Get down from there!" Pike lunged.

She hopped away and deliberately flicked a folder open with her paw.

Papers spilled across the blotter.

Lady Grey stilled, pupils narrowing.

Even she recognized Amelia's inn title—*Tumblebrook Inn*—printed across the top.

But the signatures?

Wrong.

Shaky.

Crooked.

Not Esther Farnsworth's elegant hand. Not even close.

Forgeries.

Fake deeds.

False appraisal certificates.

Property transfers that should have raised an entire blizzard of suspicion.

Lady Grey planted her paw firmly on the documents.

Pike lunged. "Don't touch that!"

She sprang aside with a disdainful flick of her tail and knocked another folder open for good measure.

Pages scattered everywhere. Evidence fanned across the desk like feathers.

Pike's face turned beet red. "You nosy little—"

He swung at her.

Lady Grey darted beneath his arm and sent a pen clattering to the floor.

The sharp sound rang into the hallway.

Too loud.

Perfectly loud.

Pike froze. "No—NO—not now—"

Footsteps pounded toward the office.

Then—

"WHAT is going on in—?"

Amelia burst in.

Pike halted mid-reach, hunched like a raccoon caught raiding the pantry. The fireplace behind him glowed, flames gnawing at half-burned papers.

Clara appeared over Amelia's shoulder and sucked in a sharp breath. "You're burning documents."

"And digging through my desk," Amelia added, voice cold enough to frost the window.

Pike sputtered. "This isn't—this isn't what it looks like!"

Lady Grey perched elegantly on the blotter, tail curled, looking utterly pleased with herself.

Clara folded her arms. "And you just happened to be rifling through Amelia's locked drawer while chasing a cat?"

Pike jabbed a finger at Lady Grey. "She's been hostile since I got here!"

Lady Grey blinked slowly.

Hostile?

No.

Simply correct.

"Mr. Pike," Amelia said, stepping forward, "what—exactly—are you doing in my office?"

Pike's gaze snapped toward the half-open window behind the desk. Amelia always cracked it for fresh air, but now he shoved it wider, letting in a blast of icy wind.

"I—listen—I don't trust this place. I don't trust—"

His eyes flicked over all three of them.

Then he moved.

"Pike, don't—!" Amelia shouted.

But he was already climbing onto the sill.

Into the blizzard.

"You can't leave," Clara cried. "The storm—"

Pike dropped down onto the snow-slick ledge. He slipped, caught the gutter pipe, and vanished into a whirling wall of white.

Amelia lunged to the window. "Pike!"

A dark blur disappeared past the porch light and into the storm.

Clara cursed. "He's running! We have to—"

A violent gust slammed the window against the frame.

The storm outside was too fierce for pursuit. Even Clara knew it.

Lady Grey hopped onto the sill, staring into the swirling snow.

Pike's scent was already being shredded and carried away by the wind.

But she knew one thing deep in her bones:

Alden Pike wasn't running away from danger.

He was running toward something...

Or someone.

And that someone was waiting for him.

Chapter 20

Midnight Pursuit

The office window still rattled under the storm's icy grip long after Pike vanished into the blizzard. For one suspended heartbeat, Amelia couldn't breathe. Snow battered the panes, wind moaned through the gutters, and the inn trembled—as if it, too, felt abandoned.

"He's going to freeze out there," Clara said, shoving her arms into her coat.

"He's going to stumble straight into more trouble," Amelia countered, grabbing her lantern and boots. Her voice wavered despite the resolve behind it. "We can't let him disappear."

A soft **mrrrp** echoed from the hall.

Lady Grey. Tail high. Pacing. Impatient.

"She's tracking him," Clara said. "We need to go. Now."

The storm roared against the walls; the house creaked like a ship fighting a furious sea. Amelia swallowed her fear, tightened her grip on the lantern, and nodded.

"Okay. We follow her. We stay together. And we don't—under any circumstances—lose sight of the inn."

They rushed to the foyer. Cold air pressed through every seam in the old door. Clara tightened her scarf; Amelia steadied her breath. Lady Grey stood at the threshold like a small, determined sentinel.

Amelia pushed the front door open.

The wind nearly tore it from her hands.

Snow blasted inward—cold and sharp as ground glass—but Lady Grey darted into the swirling white, tiny paws leaving perfect prints in the fresh drifts.

"Stay close!" Amelia shouted.

Clara nodded, teeth already chattering.

And Amelia stepped into the storm.

The cold stole her breath instantly.

Snow piled against the porch; wind curled through the eaves in wild, furious howls. The world beyond the inn dissolved into a spinning curtain of white.

But the lantern cast just enough glow to reveal the first set of tracks:

Lady Grey's delicate paw prints.

And beside them—

Pike's.

Longer.

Deeper.

Uneven—his right foot dragging.

"He's heading toward the trees," Clara shouted over the gale.

"How can you tell?" Amelia squinted through the flurries.

Clara pointed. "The trail angles downhill. Toward the lakeshore."

Toward the lake.

Amelia's stomach dipped. "No. He wouldn't—"

But he would. Cornered, desperate, terrified—Alden Pike absolutely would.

"Move!" Clara urged.

Lady Grey forged ahead with unwavering certainty, her puffed tail the only beacon in the whiteout.

"Lady Grey!" Amelia called. "Slow down!"

The cat did not slow.

They trudged through thigh-high drifts, snow clinging to their coats and eyelashes. Amelia's lantern flickered wildly in her shaking grip.

"Lantern—there!" Clara cried.

Amelia lifted it higher.

A faint shimmer of ice appeared ahead.

A darker patch of white where the lake's frozen surface began.

And Pike's footprints marched straight toward it.

"Oh, Alden..." Amelia whispered. "What have you done?"

A sudden, terrible sound sliced through the wind.

A scream.

High. Panicked. Terrified.

Pike.

Clara grabbed Amelia's arm. "Hurry!"

They ran—slipping, stumbling—hearts pounding. Lady Grey sprinted ahead, yowling a warning that cut through the storm.

When Amelia reached the lakeshore, the world tilted.

A jagged crack split the ice.

A dark fissure churned with frigid water beneath it.

And in the middle—

"Alden!" Amelia cried.

Pike thrashed, one arm barely clinging to the ice, the other flailing helplessly.

"Help!" he choked. "Please—I'm slipping—I can't—"

Clara scanned frantically. "We need something long—something to reach him!"

"The lantern pole!" Amelia yanked it free, hands trembling.

Clara tied her scarf to the end, creating a makeshift rope.

"Pike!" Amelia shouted. "Hold on!"

He slipped again, icy water dragging him downward.

Lady Grey paced the shoreline, yowling warnings.

Amelia dropped to her stomach and slid carefully onto the ice. "Clara—don't step past there! It's too thin!"

"I'm not letting you go alone," Clara said, kneeling behind her but staying on thick ice.

Amelia extended the pole. "Alden—grab it!"

He lunged—missed—floundered—sputtered.

"I can't—I can't—!"

Amelia inched forward.

The ice groaned beneath her.

Creaked.

Shifted.

One more inch and she'd fall in, too.

"Clara," she whispered, "anchor my legs."

Clara grabbed her ankles, heels digging deep into the snow.

The ice cracked again—long and splintering.

"Please!" Pike gasped.

Amelia stretched the pole farther. "Now, Alden! Now!"

He lunged once more—

Caught the scarf—

Nearly slipped again—

"No!" Amelia cried. "Hold on!"

Clara pulled. Amelia pulled.

Inches.

Slow, agonizing inches.

Pike's torso scraped over the ice. He kicked wildly, shivering hard enough to rattle bone.

One last desperate pull—

And Pike slid out onto the ice, collapsing into a sobbing heap.

Amelia couldn't breathe for a moment.

They had saved him.

Clara wrapped her coat around his trembling shoulders. "He's freezing. We need him inside."

Amelia lifted Pike's chin gently. "Alden. Can you hear me?"

His eyelids fluttered. His voice was a ragged whisper.

"You... saved me."

"Yes," Amelia said. "Now tell us—why were you running? What were you trying so hard to destroy?"

He coughed, clutching his chest. "Not... hide... destroy."

"Destroy what?" Clara pressed.

"The contracts," he gasped. "The ones tying me to the land deals. The ones Covington uncovered. He wanted to expose everything."

Clara's jaw tightened. "So Covington did know about your forgeries."

Pike nodded weakly. "He confronted me the night he arrived. Said he had proof. Said... it was time I answered for it."

Amelia studied his face.

Regret.

Fear.

Shame.

But not cruelty.

She exhaled softly. "Tell us the truth—the full truth."

Pike's breaths came in ragged gasps. "I went to the parlor earlier... during the blackout. Not to kill him. To beg him. To bargain." His throat bobbed. "But when I got there..."

Clara leaned in. "Alden—when you got there... what?"

Pike lifted his head, eyes full of raw fear.

"Someone else was in the room already."

Cold burrowed deeper into Amelia's bones. "Who?"

He shook his head violently. "I—I didn't see their face..."

The wind howled across the frozen lake.

Lady Grey hissed into the trees.

Pike clutched Amelia's sleeve.

"But I heard them whisper something... over the body."

Amelia's heart stuttered. "Alden. What did they say?"

He swallowed.

"They said..."

A violent cough wracked his body.

Amelia leaned closer.

"What. Did. They. Say?"

Pike's whisper barely carried over the blizzard.

"We bury what the lake can't hide."

Something ancient and cold slid down Amelia's spine.

Clara stared, horror widening her eyes.

Lady Grey's fur rose along her back.

And the storm closed around them, swallowing the night in a white, relentless roar.

Chapter 21

The Hidden Hand

The storm had not eased when they dragged Alden Pike back into the inn.

If anything, it had turned feral.

Wind slammed against the windows with the fury of a ship taking on water. Snow hissed through every crevice. The lights flickered—once, twice—before settling into a thin, fragile glow.

Amelia rushed to fetch blankets while Lady Grey paced in tight, furious circles around Pike's boots, tail puffed to a bristling plume.

Clara couldn't sit.

Couldn't breathe properly.

Couldn't stop hearing Pike's voice on that frozen lake.

"Someone else was in that room before me."

The words pulsed through her like a heartbeat of dread.

Pike was a liar, a forger, and a slippery opportunist—but his fear had been real. Clara trusted her instincts, and they told her one thing with absolute clarity:

Alden Pike had not killed Edward Covington.

He was tangled in the mess—absolutely—but he hadn't held

Covington beneath the lantern glow. He wasn't the shadow Clara had glimpsed during the blackout.

Which meant someone else inside Tumblebrook Inn was far more dangerous.

Clara stood near the hearth, staring into the fire as Pike shivered beneath a blanket. Amelia murmured soft reassurances, though the words barely registered.

Clara replayed the night.

The footsteps.

The shadows.

The lies.

The gaps.

Amelia approached quietly. "Clara? Are you okay?"

"No," Clara admitted, "but I'm thinking."

Amelia nodded. "Good. Because right now? Your brain is our best weapon."

Clara inhaled deeply—steadying herself—and knew exactly what she needed to do.

Clara dropped into the armchair near the coffee table. Lady Grey immediately hopped onto the armrest, close enough that her whiskers brushed Clara's sleeve—eyes sharp, like a tiny detective prepared to take notes.

Clara unfolded the worn sheet of paper she'd been carrying since the first night. Names. Times. Movements. Glaring holes.

She spread it out and traced each entry with her fingertip.

"Okay," Clara murmured. "Let's walk through this carefully."

8:12 p.m.

Lights flicker.

Covington finishes his cocoa and heads toward the parlor.

8:20 p.m.

Pike claims he went to confront Covington.

But Covington was already dead—and Pike insists he saw someone fleeing.

8:30 p.m.

Doris bursts in about the lights and the missing cookie scores.

Clara tapped the page with a slow, deliberate motion.

"That," she whispered, "never sat right."

Lady Grey tilted her head and placed a paw squarely on Doris's name.

"Yes," Clara breathed. "Exactly."

Doris's timeline had always been just a little too convenient.

Clara circled the name.

If Doris hadn't been where she said she was...

Clara's pulse quickened.

She stood abruptly, folding the timeline into her coat pocket. Lady Grey leapt down, tail raised like a banner.

"Clara?" Amelia called from the hearth. "Where are you going?"

"I need to verify something."

"Want me to come?"

Clara shook her head. "If Pike passes out again, you're the one who knows what to do. I'll be right back."

Amelia hesitated but nodded.

Clara slipped into the hall, Lady Grey gliding beside her like a silent shadow.

The inn felt cavernous in the storm—every board groaning, every lantern flickering. Clara pushed into the kitchen and lit a lantern. Its glow stretched long over the counters.

Everything at Doris's baking station was neat.

Too neat.

Flour sacks.

Sugar.

Spices aligned in perfect rows.

And then Clara saw it.

Her breath caught.

A nearly full bag labeled **Festival Bake-Off Sugar**.

That shouldn't have been possible. Doris had claimed she'd gone through pounds of sugar while prepping her gingerbread finale.

But this bag had barely been touched.

Lady Grey sniffed it, then stared at Clara, whiskers twitching pointedly.

"She lied," Clara whispered.

Her stomach twisted.

She liked Doris. She wanted to trust her. But Doris had secrets. And debts. And a "supply box" she'd refused to let anyone open.

Clara steeled herself.

She needed that box.

When Clara returned to the parlor, Doris was awake on the sofa, a blanket wrapped tightly around her trembling shoulders. Mr. Lark hovered beside her with a steaming mug of tea.

The café supply box sat near the coat rack—plain, taped, unassuming.

Clara approached it.

"Doris?" she asked gently. "I need to look inside your supply box."

Doris's teacup rattled in her hands. "M-my box? Why?"

Clara crouched beside her. "Earlier you said it was just napkins and flour. But tonight isn't the night for secrets. Please."

Doris's jaw tightened. Her breath stuttered.

Amelia joined Clara, voice soft but firm. "Doris... we need to be sure no one is in danger."

Doris wilted, shoulders sagging.

"...Go ahead."

Clara nodded and crossed the room. She cut through the tape.

The flap popped free.

Inside—

Not napkins.

Not flour.

Not supplies of any kind.

A thick leather-bound ledger filled the box, heavy and old, a faded gold butterfly embossed on its cover.

The Monarch Society emblem.

Clara's breath stilled. "Oh my..."

Amelia whispered, "Is that—?"

Clara lifted the book with trembling hands. "Their records. All of them."

Doris burst into tears.

"I didn't want any of this!" she sobbed. "My husband—his forgeries—his mistakes—they left everything on my shoulders. The Society wouldn't leave me alone. Payments... demands... debts I could never repay."

Clara knelt beside her. "Doris... why didn't you tell us?"

"I was ashamed." Doris wiped at her eyes. "And Covington—he knew. He threatened to expose everything if I didn't help him."

Clara's pulse thudded harder.

"He blackmailed you," she murmured.

Doris nodded miserably. "Yes."

Amelia and Clara exchanged a horrified, sinking look.

"Doris," Amelia whispered, "did you kill him?"

"No!" Doris cried, shaking her head violently. "I only wanted him to stop. I never touched him."

Clara took her hands gently. "Then why lie about the cookie tent?"

Doris squeezed her eyes shut. "Because... because I wasn't there. I argued with him and left. I went back to the café to calm down. I didn't want anyone to know."

Clara exhaled, tension easing—but not disappearing.

Another lie.

But not murder.

Amelia rubbed Doris's back. "Thank you for being honest."

Clara turned back to the ledger.

"May I?"

Doris nodded weakly. "Be careful... there's darkness in those pages."

Clara opened it.

Names.

Dates.

Family crests.

Transactions.

Not donations.

Bribes.

Money to bury scandals, manipulate land, silence disputes.

Page after page was a map of corruption—some of it decades old, some of it disturbingly recent.

Clara flipped deeper.

A section labeled **Ornament Archive – Restricted Entries** made her breath hitch.

"Amelia... look."

A list of stolen ornaments.

A list of fakes.

A list of missing artifacts.

"We're close," Clara whispered.

Lady Grey climbed onto Clara's shoulder, her whiskers brushing the pages as if urging her on.

Clara turned the next page—

And froze.

The handwriting shifted.

Sharper. Harsher. Fresh ink.

Amelia inhaled sharply. "How recent?"

Clara's throat tightened. "Two days."

Amelia's eyes widened. "Two days before Covington died?"

Clara nodded.

Because the entry was unmistakable:

Payment Received – E. Covington
Recipient: Monarch Society
Status: Paid in Full
Date: Two days prior to death

Clara's blood went cold.

"He was paying someone," she whispered. "Someone still tied to the Society."

Amelia's voice trembled. "He paid them... and then he was killed."

Clara stared at the ink—the fresh, damning ink.

Edward Covington – Paid in Full.

The words glistened like a signature on a death warrant.

And somewhere inside the inn...

the person who collected that payment

was still hiding in the shadows.

Chapter 22

The Cat and the Key

Lady Grey had decided the parlor rug was guilty.

Of what, exactly, she wasn't sure yet—but she knew it was hiding something.

The rug had been far too smug for days now, sprawled in front of the hearth with its oversized snowflake pattern, pretending it was just decoration and certainly not concealing any secrets.

But Lady Grey knew better.

Rugs hid things.

Keys. Crumbs. Clues.

Tonight, with the storm still raging beyond the windows and the inn's guests subdued into a tense, fearful hush, Lady Grey prowled the parlor in silence. The fire had burned down to a mellow glow, flames licking lazily at the log. Shadows danced across the walls and across the piano gleaming in the corner.

Amelia and Clara were in the study with Mr. Lark, murmuring over the Monarch ledger and found pages as if they were fragile spells. Doris had retreated to the edge of the room, pretending to nap on the settee but breathing too fast for sleep. Pike, now mostly thawed, sat near the fire with a blanket wrapped around his shoulders like a man who had looked into the lake and seen it bare its teeth.

The inn felt like it was holding its breath.

Lady Grey's whiskers quivered.

She padded to the center of the room and sat directly atop the snowflake pattern, tail curled around her paws, golden eyes bright and thoughtful.

The floorboard beneath her had once covered a hatch.

She remembered it clearly—the way the planks had lifted under her paw, the way the darkness had yawned open, the smell of dust and secrets rushing upward. They had closed it again, smoothing the rug back over the surface.

But something tugged at her now. A faint metallic scent. Familiar.

She lowered her head and sniffed.

There.

Near the edge of the rug—right where Amelia always stepped when tending the fire.

Lady Grey narrowed her eyes.

She dug.

Not in the wild, "Amelia-will-squeal" way, but with precise, determined little scoops. She bunched the rug just enough to rumple its careful placement.

Scratch.

Scritch.

Thump.

A small clink sounded.

Lady Grey froze, ears swiveling.

There it was again.

She parted the fringe with one paw.

A tiny glint of brass caught the firelight.

A key.

Lady Grey's tail shot upright, a banner of triumph.

She hooked one claw gently through the metal ring and dragged it free, letting it clatter softly onto the wood floor. The key was small, brass, familiar. She leaned down and sniffed it.

Yes.

Amelia's scent.

Old paper.

Esther Farnsworth's faint lavender.

The key from the photograph.

The same one Amelia had used to open the secret study drawer. The one Lady Grey recalled seeing on the desk amid letters and worry... and then not at all.

Humans were forever losing important things.

Lady Grey nudged the key, considering.

Why was it in the parlor? How had it worked its way beneath the rug?

Unless someone had dropped it in a hurry. Or used it where it did not belong and lost control of it.

Her gaze drifted around the room.

Pike slumped near the fire, half-asleep, wrapped in his blanket. Mr. Lark had retreated to the study. Doris lay curled on the settee, blanket pulled to her chin, her shoulders occasionally shaking. Amelia had stepped away to put on more coffee; Clara's voice drifted faintly from down the hall.

Lady Grey looked toward the piano.

It sat in the corner, polished and quiet, its lid closed, its holiday carols sleeping inside the strings. Shadows pooled beneath it—deep and dark and undisturbed.

The key's metal tasted cold when she picked it up between her teeth, but she held it anyway.

She hopped lightly off the rug and trotted toward the piano, the key dangling delicately from her mouth.

The air under the piano smelled of wood, polish, and dust.

And something else.

Cedar.

Lavender.

Pine resin.

Her old familiar trio of trouble.

Lady Grey ducked under the piano bench and then under the instrument itself. Her back brushed the underside of the frame, and the key grazed the floor as she crawled deeper into shadow.

Her whiskers brushed something solid.

A box.

Small, wooden, its corners worn smooth by years of existence. It sat snug against the wall beneath the piano, pushed so far back that no casual glance would ever notice it.

Lady Grey dropped the key with a soft clink.

She sniffed the box.

Dust.

Old polish.

The same faint scent as the letters in the study.

Esther.

And—beneath that—something sharper, almost electric.

Metal and glass and... winter air made solid.

Lady Grey's fur prickled.

A tiny keyhole waited on the front of the box, nearly invisible in the low light. She nudged the key toward it with her paw.

The brass tooth lined up perfectly.

Of course.

She batted the key with quick, precise taps. It took more effort and patience than she'd ever publicly admit, but finally—

The key slid into the keyhole.

Click.

The lock yielded.

The lid loosened a fraction.

Lady Grey sat back, heart thrumming.

This was important. She could feel it in the air—the same way she sensed Amelia's sadness before Amelia spoke it, the same way she knew exactly which guests would sneak her extra treats.

Her paw trembled slightly as she hooked her claws beneath the box lid and dragged it upward.

The hinges creaked softly.

Firelight stretched under the piano like a curious hand and brushed what lay inside.

Something glimmered.

Not with its own light, but with the illusion of it—the way glass steals flame and turns it into moving color.

Lady Grey's breath caught.

Nestled in the velvet-lined interior was an ornament unlike any she'd seen.

A crown.

Delicate, intricate, no larger than the curve of Amelia's palm, yet rich with detail—tiny peaks and arches, etched patterns curling along its surface. Flecks of emerald and ruby glass winked along the band, and in the very center—instead of a jewel—was a tiny engraved Monarch butterfly, its wings spread wide.

The crown ornament.

The one Esther had warned about in her letters.

The one Ezra had never duplicated because Covington never truly found it.

The one everyone believed had vanished with the old Monarch galas.

It had been here all along.

Under the piano.

In the parlor.

Beneath the feet of laughing guests, carolers, and clumsy cats.

Lady Grey stared at it, pupils widening until her eyes were almost entirely black.

The air around the crown felt heavier somehow, weighted with old promises and buried threats—as if the secrets sunk into its metal still whispered against the inn's foundations.

She wanted to hiss at it.

Instead, she leaned closer and sniffed.

Old metal.

Dust.

Esther's lavender.

But no fresh scent.

No one had touched this in years.

Until now.

Lady Grey placed one paw lightly against the velvet edge. The crown's cool surface caught the distant firelight, throwing a faint shimmer along the piano's underbelly.

Something shifted near the parlor doorway.

Her ears flicked.

Footsteps.

Soft.

Hesitant.

A shadow fell across the floor near the piano, stretching long and thin. Not Amelia's. Not Clara's. The angles were wrong, the silhouette smaller, shoulders bowed under invisible weight.

Lady Grey peered out from beneath the piano.

Doris Finch stood there, framed in the firelight.

Her face was blotchy from crying. Her curls were slightly flattened where they'd pressed against the settee cushion. She clutched her cardigan to her chest with one hand, staring at the piano with an expression that made Lady Grey's fur rise—a mixture of dread, longing, and something like surrender.

"Esther," Doris whispered. "You hid it here."

Lady Grey watched, utterly still.

Doris stepped closer.

Her gaze snagged on the slightly askew piano bench, the scuffed patch of floor, the faint disturbance in the rug. Her eyes followed the trail of tiny paw prints in the dust.

Then, at last, she saw the box.

And the crown.

Her breath hitched.

"Oh no," she murmured. "No, no, no..."

She dropped to her knees and leaned low, reaching under the piano. Her hand stretched out, trembling, fingers spreading toward the ornament as if pulled by a magnet.

Lady Grey hissed.

Doris flinched, eyes widening.

She saw the cat now—a pair of glowing eyes, a halo of grey fur, and one firm paw braced beside the crown.

"Lady Grey," Doris whispered, voice breaking. "Please. Please don't... don't stop me."

A strangled, humorless laugh escaped her. "Listen to me. Begging a cat. I really have lost it."

Her fingers edged closer again.

Tears dropped onto the wooden floor.

"It wasn't supposed to happen this way," she said hoarsely. "I was only supposed to hold the ledger—keep it until they finished their votes. I never meant—"

Her hand shook harder.

"I didn't want anyone to die," she breathed.

Lady Grey's heart thudded faster.

Doris's words carried the same shape as the others: *he said, they promised, it would just be leverage.* The invisible *he* who hovered behind everything.

"He said it would be a game of nerves," Doris choked out. "Just enough pressure so Alden would sign, or Covington would stay quiet, or the last of them would pay what they owed. A reminder. Not..." Her voice cracked. "...not this."

She shook her head, curls bouncing.

"And then he died. And it all—" She cut herself off, pressing her lips together.

Lady Grey understood enough.

There was someone else. Someone above Doris. Someone whose name she wouldn't say. Someone whose hands never had to touch the ornaments to move them.

But Doris's fingers were still reaching.

Still stretching toward the crown.

No.

Lady Grey's fur puffed. She pressed her paw more firmly against the velvet, staking her claim.

Then she opened her mouth and unleashed a sound she usually reserved for vacuum cleaners and unwelcome neighborhood dogs:

A full-throated, furious yowl.

It ripped through the parlor.

High.

Sharp.

Alarm.

Doris jerked back from the box as if burned, snatching her hand away in a sudden, panicked motion.

Footsteps pounded down the hall.

"Lady Grey?" Amelia's voice, already tight with worry. "What is it?"

"Grey?" Clara's voice followed, sharper, closer.

Lady Grey yowled again, louder this time, paw still braced protectively beside the crown ornament—the open box a small island of velvet and metal beneath the piano.

Doris scrambled backward, bumping into the piano bench. Her face had gone ashen, guilt and grief and terror warring in her eyes.

Amelia skidded into the parlor, lantern light spilling across the room and catching the scene in a single, breathless tableau:

Lady Grey under the piano, paw on the edge of a small open chest.

The crown ornament nestled inside, shimmering in reflected firelight.

Doris kneeling on the floor beside it, hand suspended mid-air, tear-streaked face turned toward them in shock.

Clara stopped just behind Amelia, eyes widening. "Is that...?"

Amelia's gaze darted from Doris to the box to the crown. Her breath stuttered.

And Lady Grey—

147

guardian of the inn,
finder of lost things,
feline archivist of secrets—
let out one final, ferocious yowl that seemed to vibrate through the inn's old beams.
The crown ornament had been found.
And so, at last, had one of the hands reaching for it.

Chapter 23

Broken Ornaments

Doris Finch looked impossibly small beneath the towering shadow of the grand piano.

Firelight flickered across the parlor, illuminating the tear tracks streaking her cheeks, the trembling of her shoulders, the way her fingers clutched the sides of her cardigan as if trying to keep her heart from falling out.

Clara stood frozen near the couch. Lady Grey crouched protectively beside the open chest containing the crown ornament—tail puffed, golden eyes sharp and unblinking.

Amelia stepped forward, heart pounding, and lowered herself onto the rug beside Doris.

"Doris," she said softly, "tell us what happened."

Doris pressed her lips together, fighting another sob. For a long, long moment, the only sounds in the room were the crackling fire and the distant roar of the storm outside.

Then, in a small, cracked whisper:

"I didn't kill him."

Her voice fractured like thin ice.

Amelia touched her back gently. "We believe you. But we need to understand the truth."

Doris shook her head miserably. "It wasn't supposed to happen this way. I never meant... for any of this."

Clara came closer, her voice gentler than it had been all night. "Start at the beginning."

Doris inhaled shakily, eyes shining.

"Covington came into the café three days before the festival. Said he knew about my husband's past—that he knew about the forged ornaments Charles helped sell. Said if I didn't recover them for him, he would expose everything. My husband's crimes... and mine."

Her voice broke. "I—I panicked."

Amelia frowned. "Recover them? Which ornaments?"

"The Monarch Society ones." Doris's voice barely rose above the fire's hiss. "The set Charles Finch handled years ago. Covington believed one of them—the silver starburst—was a fake. He wanted the real one."

Clara exchanged a worried look with Amelia. "And you thought Charles might have hidden the originals?"

Doris nodded. "He lied about... so much. I thought this was just one more thing."

She wiped her trembling hands on her skirt.

"Covington told me to destroy the forged ornament once I found it. Said it was the only way to protect myself. So the night of the festival... when the lights flickered... I went to confront him. I had the fake one in my apron pocket."

Amelia felt dread and sympathy coil tightly in her chest. "You wanted to get rid of it."

"Yes." Doris's voice cracked. "I thought if I destroyed it, he would stop pressuring me."

Clara knelt beside her. "And when you reached the parlor?"

Doris's eyes squeezed shut.

"He was already on the floor."

Amelia inhaled sharply.

"At first," Doris whispered, "I thought he was faking again. He... did that. Dramatic gestures, collapses, theatrics. But when I touched his shoulder..."

Her voice thinned to a thread. "He wasn't breathing."

Clara's brows knit. "You didn't see anyone else? Hear anything?"

"No," Doris whispered. "Just the storm. Just my own heartbeat. Then Lady Grey came running in, knocked over the garland, and I panicked. I fled."

Lady Grey yowled indignantly under the piano.

Amelia pressed a hand over her heart. The timeline settled—but the picture remained fractured.

"You didn't poison the cocoa," she said gently.

"No. No." Doris shook her head fiercely. "The mug was already on the floor when I got there. Whatever happened to him... happened before I arrived."

Clara exhaled. "So the poisoner struck before any arguments. Before you ever reached him."

"Yes," Doris whispered. "Whoever did it was ahead of all of us."

A tense silence fell.

Not Doris.

Not Pike.

Not Ezra.

Someone else had been in that parlor.

Someone who knew Covington's patterns, his vulnerabilities, his secrets.

Someone still inside the inn.

Amelia straightened slowly, mind racing.

A thought tugged at her—something Ezra said upstairs. Something she'd brushed past but now blazed like a lantern.

The receipt.

The supplies.

"These weren't for destroying ornaments," she murmured.

Clara blinked. "What?"

"Ezra didn't use those materials to hide evidence," Amelia said.

"He used them because he's a carver. A restorer. He was fixing the original ornaments, not destroying them."

Clara's eyes widened as understanding clicked into place. "So he was helping Covington preserve the evidence."

"Exactly." Amelia nodded. "Ezra wasn't altering the originals—he was repairing them."

Doris gasped softly. "Then the duplicates..."

"...were meant to replace the originals," Amelia finished. "So Covington could keep the real ones safe."

Clara let out a slow breath. "Which means the originals we've found... the ones that were damaged..."

Amelia nodded grimly. "They've been tampered with—but not by Ezra."

Doris clapped a trembling hand over her mouth. "So the killer is still trying to destroy the evidence."

"And still inside the inn," Clara murmured.

Amelia rose to her feet, pulse thundering.

Her gaze swept the parlor.

The piano.

The firelit walls.

The shifting shadows.

Another memory surfaced—something Covington had been holding that first night, something he treasured almost irrationally.

"Wait," Amelia breathed. "Where's the music box?"

Clara's head snapped up. "What?"

"The music box," Amelia repeated, scanning the room. "Covington kept it with him everywhere. He dropped it the night the lights flickered. We found it again in the study. But now—"

It wasn't on the mantle.

Not on the table.

Not by his coat.

Not near his belongings.

Gone.

Lady Grey's ears flattened.

Clara stood abruptly. "Someone took it."

Amelia swallowed hard.

Covington had hidden something inside that music box—a folded note, a code, a final clue.

And now it was missing.

Taken in the chaos.

Taken deliberately.

By someone who didn't want the truth found.

By someone who knew how close they were getting.

"Clara," Amelia whispered, "we're not done. Not even close."

Clara nodded slowly, fear blooming behind her eyes. "Someone is still working against us."

"Someone," Amelia murmured, "who doesn't want the truth coming out."

Outside, the storm slammed against the inn with renewed fury.

Inside, the parlor felt too quiet.

Too still.

Too watched.

Chapter 24

The Melody Returns

The music box began to play at exactly twelve minutes past midnight.

Clara knew the time because she'd been staring at the parlor mantel clock for the last hour, unable to sleep, her mind circling the same tangled knots—Covington, the ledger, Doris's confession, Ezra's duplicates, Pike's panic, the crown under the piano, and the invisible hand pulling all of them toward some dark center.

Amelia had drifted into a light doze on the couch, Lady Grey curled protectively against her hip like a furry sentry. Pike and Doris lay tucked into makeshift cots in the sitting room. Ezra, still pale and exhausted, rested near the hearth wrapped in a blanket.

Clara alone remained restless.

She paced softly around the parlor, careful not to wake Amelia, when a faint chiming melody slipped down through the ceiling.

She stopped mid-step.

Not the wind.

Not a draft.

Not the old plumbing humming to itself.

Music.

A delicate, tinkling waltz. Slow. Precise. Mournful.

Clara's breath caught.

She knew that melody.

Covington's music box.

The same tune that had played the night he died.

The same music box Amelia had only just realized was missing.

Her heartbeat kicked into a sprint.

She lifted her gaze toward the ceiling. The notes were faint but clear, drifting from above.

From the attic.

Lady Grey's head snapped up. The cat slid off the couch in one silent motion, ears forward, pupils dilating.

"You hear it too," Clara whispered.

Lady Grey brushed against her leg, tail flicking with purpose.

Clara swallowed, grabbed the lantern from beside the hearth, and steadied her breath.

"Okay," she murmured, mostly to herself. "We're doing this. Again."

She took a step toward the staircase.

Lady Grey trotted ahead without hesitation, leading the way.

The house creaked softly as Clara climbed the steep attic stairs, each footfall muffled by dust and by the padded hush of the storm pressing against the roof. The higher she went, the clearer the tune became.

Soft.

Insistent.

As if each note were a fingertip tapping at the edge of a secret.

At the top, she paused on the landing.

The attic stretched out before her in dim, sloping shadows. Her lantern's small circle of light barely reached the far corners. Crates and trunks loomed like sleeping shapes under the rafters. The storm thrashed against the roof in angry bursts.

Lady Grey slipped forward, tail low, nose twitching as she traced along trunks and boxes, following scents Clara couldn't begin to name.

The melody floated from the far end of the room—behind the old wardrobe and the heap of festival decorations Amelia had dragged out weeks ago.

Clara lifted the lantern higher.

"Hello?" she whispered, hating how thin her voice sounded.

No reply.

Just the slow, mechanical turn of the tune.

She rounded the wardrobe—

—and gasped.

Mr. Lark sat on the floor.

His knees were drawn to his chest, shoulders hunched, glasses slipping down his nose. His hands shook violently.

In those hands—

Covington's music box.

He was winding it in slow, uneven turns, his gaze fixed on some point far beyond the room.

"Mr. Lark?" Clara breathed.

He jolted. The winder slipped from his fingers, the melody warbling before reasserting itself in a wavering sway.

"Clara," he whispered hoarsely. "You shouldn't be here."

Lady Grey padded forward and sat, wrapping her tail neatly around her paws, eyes fixed on him with a measured, assessing stare.

Clara kept her voice soft as she stepped closer. "I heard the music. I came to see who had the box."

Mr. Lark's eyes glistened. In the attic's lantern light, he looked older than he ever had downstairs—edges frayed, grief hollowing his face.

"I didn't think anyone would hear it," he murmured. "Not over the storm."

Clara took another step forward. "Please... talk to me."

He lowered his gaze to the box in his hands.

"It's strange," he said, voice barely above a whisper. "He never let me touch it. Not once. Even when we were boys."

Clara blinked. "Boys?"

Mr. Lark's mouth trembled.

"Yes," he said. "Edward and I..." He swallowed. "We shared a mother."

Clara's heart stuttered.

"You mean—you're siblings?"

"Half-brothers," Mr. Lark whispered. "Our mother remarried when he was young and I was an infant. Edward was raised by her first husband's family. I was the afterthought." He let out a shaky breath. "And he never forgave either of us for that."

Lady Grey's ears twitched.

Clara's thoughts spun. "You're saying Covington... resented you?"

"Deeply," Mr. Lark said. "He blamed me for everything. For her death. For her debts. For every hardship he claimed had marked his early years." His fingers traced the edge of the box. "And yet... I loved him. Even when he refused to acknowledge me."

The lantern flame fluttered.

"You came to the inn to confront him," Clara said softly. "About the past."

He nodded once, shoulders curling inward.

"I came to stop him," he whispered. "Not to kill him. To stop him. He was about to ruin everything."

Clara's chest tightened. "Ruin what?"

Mr. Lark opened the box fully and brushed his thumb along a faint carving inside the lid—two initials, softened with age.

E.C. & R.L.

Brothers.

"He made that when he was twelve," Mr. Lark said, voice shaking. "Before he decided we weren't family anymore."

Clara felt a painful tug behind her ribs.

"Why hide that?" she asked quietly. "Why pretend you weren't related?"

"Because he wanted to be seen as self-made. Independent. Untied to anyone," Mr. Lark said. "And because he carried one mistake he could never outrun."

Clara waited.

"He lied," Mr. Lark whispered. "In one of his earliest big appraisals, decades ago. Do you remember the scandal of the stolen Monarch ornaments?"

Clara nodded slowly. "The case that nearly ended his career."

"He didn't just appraise the stolen pieces," Mr. Lark said. "He suspected they were forgeries and looked the other way. He wanted the commission. The fame. He wanted the story." His voice frayed. "And when the truth came out, he needed someone to blame."

Clara's throat tightened. "You."

Mr. Lark nodded once.

"I was young. I cataloged pieces for him. That was all." He swallowed. "But when the scandal broke, he let everyone believe I had mishandled the records. He let them think I was the incompetent one. He sacrificed my reputation to save his own."

Horror and heartbreak knotted together in Clara's chest.

"You came for justice," she murmured.

"Or closure," he said. "I don't know which."

The music box's melody hit a delicate, lilting high note, then faltered. Mr. Lark wound it again, fingers trembling.

"I didn't poison him, Clara," he said, looking up sharply. "I swear to you. I argued with him. I demanded an apology. But he laughed. Called me weak. Said I was still nothing." His shoulders sagged. "I left in anger. But he was alive when I walked away."

Clara held his gaze.

He wasn't slick or evasive or calculated.

He was simply shattered.

She swallowed. "Mr. Lark... the poison was in the cocoa he drank before you ever reached the parlor."

His eyes widened in shock.

"Then whoever poisoned him..." he whispered.

"...did so before either of you went in," Clara finished.

Lady Grey moved closer, sniffing lightly at his coat. He reached out with unsteady fingers and stroked the top of her head.

"She always liked him," he said, voice rough. "Every time he visited the shop, she followed him between the shelves."

Clara rested a hand gently on his shoulder. "We don't think you're the killer," she said. "But we need to know one thing."

He nodded, eyes wet.

"Who else knew you and Covington were meeting tonight?"

Mr. Lark closed his eyes, as if listening backward in time.

"I don't know," he said finally. "But—" He hesitated, voice thinning. "I felt it, Clara. Someone else was up here earlier."

Clara's pulse jumped. "Who?"

"I don't know," he repeated. "When I first came up... the shadows moved. And one of the crates was still swaying. Someone slipped out before I rounded the wardrobe."

A fresh chill slid down Clara's spine.

She raised the lantern, sweeping its light across the far end of the attic. Boxes. Old trunks. The sloping curve of the rafters. Nothing moved now.

But the skin at the back of her neck prickled.

A faint draft brushed past her cheek.

The music box's melody sputtered and slowed, its last notes trembling like a breath held too long.

Lady Grey's tail puffed to its full size.

Clara swallowed and took one cautious step toward the darker corner behind the wardrobe.

"Hello?" she called softly.

Silence.

The attic held its breath.

Then—

CREEEEAAAAK.

A floorboard groaned from the far side of the wardrobe. Not under Clara.

Not under Mr. Lark.

Not beneath Lady Grey.

Someone else was up here.

Chapter 25

Whiskers in the Rafters

L ady Grey did not like the attic.

It smelled of dust and old wood and the sort of forgotten things humans insisted on keeping for sentimental reasons but never actually looked at. The beams creaked suspiciously. Shadows clung to the rafters like cobwebs that had grown a little too ambitious. And worst of all, humans never seemed to notice the very obvious fact that the attic had far too many hiding places for comfort.

But if danger insisted on slinking around in the rafters, then so would she.

Keeping her belly low and her paws silent, Lady Grey crept along a beam above Clara and Mr. Lark. Her balance, of course, was impeccable—unmatched, really—and she peered down at the humans with cool feline judgment. Below, Clara held her lantern high, the trembling glow casting warm orange pools across stacked crates and trunks. Mr. Lark still clutched Covington's music box, his expression shaken and worn.

The melody had finally stuttered into silence, but its last shivering notes still lingered in the air like something listening.

Clara whispered into the shadows.

"Who's there?"

The attic answered with silence... and one long, low creak from the far corner.

Lady Grey's ears snapped toward the sound.

There.

Behind the wardrobe.

Near the vent.

The scent hit her next—sharp metal from the grates, oil from tools, and beneath that, something new:

Leather.

Snow.

Varnish.

And lacquer.

Not Ezra.

Not Pike.

Not Doris.

Not Mr. Lark.

Someone else.

Someone she didn't know.

Lady Grey narrowed her eyes and eased forward along the beam. Clara, naturally, could see nothing beyond the lantern's timid circle of light—but Lady Grey's vision sliced through the gloom like a paw through wrapping paper. She followed the new scent toward the rafters above the wardrobe.

At first, nothing moved.

Then she saw it.

A gloved hand reached through the slats of the attic vent—fingers moving with quiet, practiced intent as they loosened the bolts.

One twist.

Two twists.

Soft metal squeaks.

Lady Grey's fur puffed from tail to whisker.

This was not normal "I'm just helping with the ventilation" behavior.

This was sneaky vent behavior.

The hand withdrew briefly, then returned holding something small and square—an envelope or folded bundle. It angled toward the vent, pushing something inside... or pulling something out. Hard to say.

Lady Grey's whiskers twitched sharply.

Absolutely not.

She crouched low, wiggled once, and launched herself.

She landed just above the vent grille, claws scraping lightly across the beam.

The gloved hand jerked in panic, dropping a loose screw. It pinged off the vent, bounced across the attic floor, and rolled into the lantern's pool of light.

Clara flinched.

"What was that?"

Lady Grey snarled and slammed both paws against the slats.

The grille rattled violently.

The hand darted backward—but not before the glove peeled away just enough for a flash of bare skin.

A pale wrist.

A dark sleeve.

And a faint smear of blue paint along the cuff.

Lady Grey's mind sharpened.

Paint.

Not Pike's neat ink smudges.

Not Mr. Lark's parchment dust.

Paint thick and oily—like the kind used on carved ornaments.

Her eyes widened.

Ezra.

But no—the scent was wrong. Ezra always smelled of pine shavings, coffee, and the quiet that comes from working alone.

Except... Ezra had mentioned someone else.

Help.

Occasional help.

An assistant.

An apprentice.

The hand vanished into the vent.

Lady Grey hissed, crouched low, and stared into the narrow opening.

For a heartbeat, a face stared back.

Young.

Dark hair.

Wind-burned cheeks.

Ezra's apprentice.

She recognized him now in flashes—hood up at the festival, stacking Ezra's crates, lingering at the edges of booths, blending into the crowd in a way humans rarely noticed...

...but cats always did.

He didn't belong in her attic.

He didn't belong in the inn's vents.

And he definitely did not belong anywhere near the ornaments.

Their eyes met.

He jolted backward and scrambled away from the shaft.

"Someone's up there," Clara whispered urgently. "Grey's found them."

Lady Grey darted along the beam toward a support post, mapping the fastest route down.

Boards creaked above the wardrobe—the intruder was moving fast, heading toward the attic hatch.

Lady Grey wouldn't allow that.

She sprang from the beam to a crate, from the crate to the floor, landing with perfect feline precision. Clara and Mr. Lark turned just as another sound echoed behind them—

Bootsteps.

Fast.

Panicked.

Fleeing.

"Stop!" Clara shouted, sweeping the lantern toward the far corner.

The light caught the blur of a dark coat slipping behind stacked trunks.

Ezra's apprentice—Rory, Clara had mentioned once in the kitchen—bolted for the hatch.

"What are you doing up here?" Clara cried. "Hey! Stop!"

He didn't answer.

He lunged for the attic stairs.

Lady Grey shot across the floor like a furry arrow. Dust scattered beneath her paws as she intercepted him at the top step.

He leapt over her—impressively, she grudgingly noted—but she sprang upward, claws flashing, and snagged his boot.

He stumbled, grabbing a beam to steady himself.

"Get away, cat!" he hissed.

Lady Grey hissed right back.

Her claws caught the hem of his scarf—a thick wool thing coiled tightly around his neck. The fabric tugged. Stretched. Strained.

She held on.

He yanked forward.

She yanked backward.

The scarf slipped free, whipping off his collar entirely.

He shoved off the beam, half-slid, half-fell down the stairs, boots thundering onto the main floor.

"Clara!" Mr. Lark gasped. "He's running!"

"I see that!" Clara said, rushing to the hatch.

But Lady Grey stayed where she was.

Because something soft and tangled lay beneath her paw.

She shook her claws free, letting the scarf tumble to the floor.

Dark wool.

Still damp from melted snow.

Carrying the intruder's scent—varnish, cold air, and the same faint tobacco note she had caught earlier near the parlor.

But it wasn't the smell that made her fur rise.

It was the symbol.

Embroidered at the frayed end of the scarf, stitched in gold thread:

A butterfly.

Not a charming, decorative butterfly.

A Monarch butterfly.

Wings spread.

Body slender.

Curved antennae.

The emblem she'd seen in ledgers, in carvings, in secrets buried deep beneath Tumblebrook's surface.

Lady Grey stared at it, fur bristling.

Ezra's apprentice was no innocent helper.

He was a Monarch spy.

Sent into Tumblebrook under the guise of an artist's assistant.

Sent to recover the ornaments.

Sent to snake through vents and shadows while everyone suspected the wrong people.

Lady Grey lowered her head and sniffed the emblem, imprinting it into memory.

Below them, voices erupted—Clara shouting, doors slamming, footsteps scattering as guests scrambled awake.

But up here, in the dim attic, the revelation thrummed like a live wire.

Lady Grey placed one paw firmly on the scarf, claws lightly extended, claiming it like a captured trophy.

The Monarch butterfly gleamed faintly in the lantern light.

Proof.

A hidden hand had finally slipped.

And Lady Grey—guardian of the inn, defender of the truth—now held a piece of it in her claws.

Chapter 26

The Final Ornament

The chase moved through the inn like a gust of wind that had finally forced its way past the walls.

Footsteps thundered down the stairs.

Clara's voice rang through the hallway—sharp, steady, in control.

Mr. Lark called for the intruder to stop.

And beneath the chaos, beneath the storm still rattling every windowpane, a cold, clear certainty settled over Amelia.

This was it.

The moment all the scattered clues had been circling.

She snatched the lantern from the parlor table and rushed into the hall, nearly losing her footing on the polished floorboards. Lady Grey shot past Clara's heels like grey lightning—tail puffed, paws skidding as she launched herself after the fleeing apprentice.

"Down the hall!" Clara shouted. "Toward the library!"

Amelia followed the sound of it all—the frantic boots, Clara's quicker steps, the feather-soft thuds of Lady Grey's paws—everything funneling toward the back wing of the inn.

The lantern swung wildly in her hand, casting frantic, leaping shadows along the staircase and across the portraits lining the corridor. Old familiar faces—her grandmother's among them—watched in solemn silence, as if bearing witness.

"Clara, be careful!" Amelia called breathlessly as the storm shrieked outside and the floor trembled with a sudden gust.

Clara didn't answer.

The library door banged open ahead.

Amelia ran harder.

She reached the threshold just in time to see the apprentice skid behind a wall of tall bookshelves, sending a stack of atlases tumbling to the floor. His coat was torn where Lady Grey had raked him. His scarf—the one embroidered with the Monarch butterfly—was gone.

Clara stood in the center of the room, between him and the only exit.

"Don't move," she said, voice steady despite the tremor in her hands.

The apprentice—Rory, Ezra's quiet, almost invisible assistant—froze.

Amelia stepped up beside Clara and raised the lantern. Warm light painted Rory's face in gold and shadow. Up close, he looked younger than she'd thought—barely older than Clara. His eyes darted between them, searching every corner for an escape that simply didn't exist.

Along the far shelf, Lady Grey slunk into place, tail tip ticking back and forth, ready to spring again if he tried.

"Rory," Amelia said, keeping her voice gentle but firm, "you need to stop running."

His Adam's apple bobbed as he swallowed. "You don't understand."

Clara's tone hardened. "Then explain it. Because we're fresh out of patience."

For a heartbeat, his body coiled as if he might bolt again. His fingers flexed. His breath came in short, tight bursts.

Then his shoulders sagged.

He let out a hollow exhale. "I never wanted it to come to this," he whispered.

"Then start with the truth," Amelia said.

Rory's gaze flicked toward the door, then to Lady Grey, who crouched lower, pupils widening. There was nowhere left to go. Nowhere to hide.

He backed into the bookcase behind him, the shelves trembling slightly with the impact.

"I didn't choose the Monarch Society," he said. "I was born into it."

The words dropped into the library like stones.

Clara's eyes widened. "You're a descendant?"

Rory nodded once, jaw tight. "My grandfather was one of the last active members. The Society never died—it just went quiet. Waiting. Watching."

Amelia felt the lantern grow heavier in her hand. "Waiting for what?"

"For the town to forget," Rory said. "For new faces to move in. For old records to be 'cleaned up.' For the people who remembered the truth to grow tired or die." His voice roughened. "For a chance to rebuild."

Clara drew in a sharp breath. "So that's what this is. Monarch version two-point-oh."

Rory's gaze snapped to hers. "Not a revival. A rise. Quieter. Smarter. With new leadership, new funding, new members. We were close." His hands clenched at his sides. "And Covington threatened that."

Amelia's heart thudded painfully. "He discovered the plan."

"He discovered everything," Rory said bitterly. "The ledger. The ornaments. Our messages. He wasn't cautious—he cornered people, hinted at what he knew, bragged that he had the crown. He threatened to go public." His expression twisted. "He would have burned us all to the ground."

Lady Grey let out a low hiss.

Clara's voice dropped to a cold whisper. "So you poisoned him."

Rory flinched—but he didn't deny it.

Amelia's stomach turned. "You killed him."

"I didn't want to," Rory snapped, then lowered his voice. "But he gave me no choice. If he exposed the Society's rebirth, everything my family worked for was gone. We'd be ruined. And you—" he glanced at the floor, jaw tightening, "—you wouldn't have a clue what poison was drifting back into this town."

Clara took a step closer, heat in her eyes. "You are the poison."

He recoiled like the words had struck him.

Amelia's tone turned to ice. "Why the ornaments? Why the crown piece?"

Rory's gaze flickered. "Because the crown is the key."

"To what?" Clara demanded.

"To the Society's charter," Rory said. "A symbol, yes, but also a code. It was crafted to hold a map—an encoded route to the original vault. Our archives. Our financial records. Our debts. Our leverage. Whoever holds the crown holds the way in."

Amelia's throat went dry.

"And Covington found it," Rory went on. "Or thought he had. He knew it could expose everything—past and future. He started waving that danger around like a torch in a dry forest."

Clara's jaw tightened. "So you killed him."

Rory swallowed. "I silenced him."

"And the poison?" Amelia asked.

Rory's face twisted. "Foxglove derivative. Easy enough to extract. Easier to mix into cocoa. That's why I pushed to 'help' with the café deliveries." A humorless half-smile tugged at his mouth. "Doris never suspected her powdered sugar wasn't just sugar."

Clara's hands clenched at her sides. "You planned this."

"I planned to keep my family safe," Rory shot back. "That's all."

Amelia's voice sharpened. "And you murdered a man to do it."

Rory's chest rose and fell in jagged breaths. "He wasn't supposed to die so quickly. I thought the dose would only make him sick, buy us time. I didn't intend—"

"Don't," Clara cut in. "Don't dress this up for us."

Rory's expression crumpled, then hardened again.

"I didn't want to kill him," he said quietly, "but I did. And I'd still choose my family over a man who spent his life profiting off other people's secrets."

Amelia's pulse hammered. "And now? What were you doing in the vent?"

He hesitated only a moment.

"I was looking for the crown," he said. "It's the last piece I need. Without it, the Society splinters again." His stare fixed on Amelia. "You know where it is."

Amelia felt every gaze in the room turn to her—Clara's, sharp and worried; Lady Grey's, steady and sure.

"Amelia—" Clara began quietly.

Amelia drew in a slow breath.

"Yes," she said. "I know."

Rory's eyes widened. Hunger and fear tangled together in his expression. "Give it to me and I'll leave," he said. "I'll disappear. Tumblebrook can go back to pretending the Monarch Society is just a rumor. You won't hear from us again."

The lantern flame fluttered in a draft.

Amelia slipped a hand into her coat.

Clara caught her arm. "Don't," she whispered. "You don't owe him anything."

Amelia squeezed her hand in brief reassurance. Then she withdrew the small velvet-lined box.

The crown ornament glimmered faintly from its nest—delicate and intricate, glass and metal catching the lantern's glow in shards of red and green and gold.

Rory inhaled as if he were seeing something sacred. "That belongs to my family," he whispered.

Amelia met his gaze.

"No," she said, calm and sure. "It belongs to the truth."

Rory went still.

"This ornament," Amelia continued, "is proof of everything the Monarch Society was—and everything it's trying to become again. It's the key to the vault and the ledger of every crime you're so desperate to bury. Covington didn't die so you could keep playing the same game in the shadows."

Rory's face twisted, outrage crowding out fear. "You don't understand what will happen if this gets out."

"Yes," Amelia said softly. "I do."

She closed the box.

Firmly.

"We're done letting the past control this town."

Clara stepped in closer, chin lifted. "You're not taking anything else from this inn. Not the ornaments, not the records, and not our future."

The floorboards creaked under Rory's shifting weight. His hands fisted at his sides. His jaw clenched so tightly a muscle jumped in his cheek.

Lady Grey's golden eyes narrowed to slits.

Before Rory could speak again, a new sound slipped into the library.

Not the wind.

Not the crackle of the fire.

A thin, rising wail, muffled at first, then growing clearer.

Sirens.

Clara's head snapped toward the window. "The storm—"

"It's breaking," Amelia breathed. "Someone must've reached Sheriff Daniels. The roads are clearing."

Rory stiffened, the blood draining from his face.

He glanced at the door.

At the window.

At the ceiling vent.

Back to the crown box in Amelia's hands.

Trapped.

Amelia held the box to her chest, the weight of it suddenly feeling less like a burden and more like resolve.

"No more running," she said quietly.

The sirens grew louder, their rising wail threading through the storm.

For the first time all night, real hope sparked behind Clara's eyes.

Rory's breathing turned sharp and uneven. Every line of his body screamed tension and regret and the last flailing edge of defiance.

Lady Grey let out a low growl, muscles bunched to leap if he tried anything.

And then—

Through the thinning storm and swirling snow, a flash of red and blue washed across the windowpanes.

Help had finally reached Tumblebrook Inn.

And so had the moment of reckoning.

Chapter 27

Christmas Morning at Tumblebrook

Snow always arrived slowly in Tumblebrook, like a guest too polite to knock. This morning was no different.

The storm had finally exhausted itself overnight, leaving behind a soft, shimmering stillness that coated the rooftops, the fir trees, even the inn's porch steps in crystalline quiet. Pale gold sunlight edged over the horizon, turning the drifts into blankets of glitter.

Inside Tumblebrook Inn, the house felt as though it had finally exhaled.

Tension drained from the walls.

Heat seeped back into the floorboards.

The scent of cinnamon and pine curled warmly through the parlor.

Clara sat at the long table, both hands wrapped around a mug of peppermint coffee. Steam curled upward like a ribbon, warming her face. After the night they'd survived, *warm* counted for something.

Across the room, Sheriff Daniels finished scribbling in his battered notebook. His mustache twitched in irritation—he despised being snowed in, and he despised being late to a crime scene even more.

At least now he was here.

And Rory—Monarch's hidden apprentice and the inn's unexpected villain—sat handcuffed on the sofa beside a deputy, staring blankly at the Christmas tree as if it had personally offended him.

Clara sipped again. Her nerves were still humming, but peppermint dulled the sharpest edges.

Amelia sat across from her with Lady Grey curled like a furry heating pad in her lap, a soft, steady purr vibrating through the room.

Doris Finch dabbed her eyes with a lace handkerchief, relieved beyond words to be free of suspicion. Mr. Lark sat stiffly near the fire, twisting his own handkerchief between anxious fingers.

Ezra leaned against the mantel, cane at his side. He looked older today—worn down by the knowledge that he had unknowingly welcomed a wolf into his workshop.

"I'll never forgive myself," he murmured. "I should've seen it."

Amelia touched his arm gently. "Ezra, trusting someone isn't a crime."

His voice cracked with quiet grief. "It nearly was."

Sheriff Daniels cleared his throat loudly, splitting the tension like an axe splitting firewood.

"Well," he said, snapping his notebook shut, "looks like we've got what we need. Poisoning. Tampering with evidence. Fraud. Trespassing. And a good handful of break-ins for good measure."

Rory stiffened, though the defiant tilt of his chin remained.

"Deputy," Daniels said, "take him out to the cruiser."

As Rory was escorted out, Lady Grey's tail flicked in a thoroughly satisfied arc.

The front door closed behind him, and for the first time since the storm began, the inn was quiet.

Daniels turned back to the group with a gruff sigh. "Now then. Someone wanna tell me what in the shiny candy cane happened here?"

Clara looked at Amelia.

Amelia looked at Clara.

They both nodded—

—and told him everything.

The Truth, Laid Bare

It took nearly an hour to unravel the entire story—

the ornaments,

the codes,

the cellar vault,

the music box,

the ledgers,

the poison,

and the Monarch Society's plans to rise again.

Sheriff Daniels listened with growing disbelief, eyebrows climbing higher and higher until Clara feared they might detach entirely.

When they finished, he let out a long, wheezing whistle.

"Well," he said, adjusting his hat, "I've heard of secret clubs, but this takes the gingerbread house."

Doris sniffed. "Am I... in trouble?"

Daniels shrugged. "You're guilty of one thing: terrible judgment and a flair for dramatics."

Doris pressed a hand to her heart. "Oh, bless you."

Ezra sagged with relief. Mr. Lark wiped at the corners of his eyes.

Amelia leaned forward. "Sheriff... what happens next?"

"We handle business the same way we always do," Daniels replied. "With a little more honesty and a lot fewer masked societies." He tucked his notebook under his arm. "Ornaments stay in evidence. Except—"

His gaze shifted to Lady Grey.

"Except the one she knocked free. That one stays here. Cat ownership, apparently."

Lady Grey preened proudly, whiskers forward.

Clara couldn't stop smiling.

"Merry Christmas, folks," Daniels said as he headed for the door. "Try real hard to avoid any crimes till tomorrow."

Clara wasn't optimistic, but she appreciated the sentiment.

By midmorning, the inn had settled into calm. Guests drifted back to their rooms. Snowplows carved a narrow path through town. Amos from the general store arrived in his dented pickup, offering rides with his usual mixture of cheer and sarcasm.

Amelia insisted everyone eat before collapsing from exhaustion. But Doris stood and smoothed her apron with stubborn resolve.

"We're going to the café," she declared. "No arguments. It's Christmas morning. People need somewhere warm to go."

"You need to rest," Clara protested.

Doris waved a dismissive hand. "Nonsense. Nothing cures shock like blueberry brioche."

Clara exchanged a look with Amelia.

...She wasn't wrong.

Within the hour, the group trudged into town through soft piles of snow—Lady Grey perched on Amelia's shoulder, surveying her kingdom.

Lights twinkled beneath frosted eaves. Snow-dusted wreaths hung from lampposts. The world felt clean again, as if the storm had scrubbed the night's darkness from every surface.

The café was bustling in a cheerful, small-town way. Dr. Hazelwood poured cocoa by the urnful. Mrs. Kendrick handed out knitted ornaments she'd been storing since July. Children chased each other around the tables, slipping on their socks and cackling with delight.

Clara helped Doris set out trays of cinnamon buns and bread pudding. Amelia carried cranberry scones to a corner table. Ezra warmed his hands around a mug of tea by the window. Mr. Lark and Doris shared a tentative smile—two people offering forgiveness without fully speaking it.

Sheriff Daniels arrived later for cocoa, pausing at Clara's shoulder.

"Good nose for trouble," he said.

"I call it intuition," Clara replied.

Lady Grey claimed her usual windowsill, watching the snowfall with regal approval.

Clara reached out and scratched behind her ears. "It's finally over," she whispered.

Lady Grey purred in agreement.

By late afternoon, Clara and Amelia returned to the inn—full, warm, and more at peace than they'd been in days. The fire crackled. Carols hummed softly from the old radio. Mulled cider filled the air with cloves and citrus.

It felt like Christmas at last.

Clara stepped into the front hall—

—and froze.

A small parcel sat neatly on the doormat.

Wrapped in cream paper.

Tied with red twine.

No footprints in the slush.

No knock.

No sound of anyone leaving.

Just the parcel.

"Amelia?" she called.

Amelia hurried over with Lady Grey trotting at her heels. "What is it?"

Clara bent and lifted the package.

No name.

No address.

Just a seal pressed into the paper.

A butterfly.

The Monarch butterfly.

Amelia inhaled sharply. "Clara..."

"I know," Clara whispered.

Lady Grey's fur prickled along her spine.

"Open it?" Amelia asked.

Clara nodded and passed it to her.

Amelia untied the twine, peeled back the paper, and opened the small box inside.

Clara leaned closer.

Nestled in the velvet—

a single glass snowflake ornament,

hand-cut,

delicate,

perfect.

Beside it lay a note on stiff parchment.

Elegant script curled across the page:

For those who guard the truth.

Merry Christmas.

Clara stared.

Amelia stared.

Lady Grey hissed softly—

not in fear.

In recognition.

This wasn't a threat.

It wasn't a warning.

Not exactly.

It was a message.

A promise.

And a reminder—

that Tumblebrook's secrets were far from finished.

Not even close.

Chapter 28

Lady Grey's Gift

Lady Grey did not trust mysterious packages.

Packages meant surprises.

Surprises meant unfamiliar scents.

Unfamiliar scents meant possible danger.

And also—occasionally—catnip.

But usually danger.

Especially those found nestled inside other packages.

So when Clara carried the cream-wrapped, red-twined parcel into the parlor and set it on the low table near the fire, Lady Grey watched it with narrowed eyes from her throne—otherwise known as Amelia's shoulder. Her tail flicked once. Twice. Three times.

Amelia was still reading the note aloud, voice soft and thoughtful, while Clara hovered behind her like a second shadow.

Lady Grey allowed them a respectable thirty seconds of human contemplation.

Then she leapt.

She landed squarely in front of the package, fur settling in a dignified ripple.

A collective gasp fluttered through the room.

"Lady Grey—!" Clara lunged forward.

Amelia, too.

Too late.

Lady Grey hooked one claw beneath the twine and tugged. The ribbon snapped with a satisfying *twip*, and the paper sagged open like a defeated snowdrift.

Clara sighed. "She's opening it."

Amelia's mouth tipped into a smile. "Of course she is. It was only a matter of time."

Lady Grey ignored them both.

She nosed the paper aside and worked with delicate precision—present-opening expertise far superior to anything human hands could achieve. When the lid of the box peeked out, she tapped it once, twice, then flipped it open with a confident whack of her paw.

The scent reached her first—clean, metallic, faintly sweet.

Then the shape.

A small ornament rolled gently across the table and came to rest against her front paw.

Lady Grey's whiskers flared.

It was a cat.

A silver cat.

Sleek and elegant, tail curled in a perfect loop like a question mark. Firelight scattered in tiny gleams along its polished sides. Fine etchings traced its back—swirls like winter wind, drifting snow, something older still. Something that tugged at instinct the way birds on windowsills or dusty secret corners always did.

Clara drew in a breath. "It's... a cat."

"A silver cat," Amelia murmured, enchanted.

Lady Grey approved of their observation.

She batted the ornament gently, watching light ripple over its surface. It chimed faintly—a soft, bell-like ring, as if a snowflake had struck ice and left the sound behind.

But the ornament wasn't alone.

Lady Grey leaned closer and spotted a small folded slip of paper nestled in the padding. She hooked a paw behind it, scooped it free, and dropped it onto the table where the humans could finally be useful.

Clara picked it up and unfolded it.

Her breath hitched. "It's another note."

Lady Grey waited, tail tip twitching.

Clara read aloud:

For those who remember what truly matters.

The fire crackled. Snow tapped at the windows in soft, steady patterns. The parlor seemed to hold its breath for a beat.

Amelia reached out and stroked Lady Grey's head. "I think that gift was meant for you."

Lady Grey purred—loudly.

Of course it was meant for her.

Who else could it possibly be for?

She was the heart of the inn.

The protector of Amelia.

The finder of clues.

The unmasker of cowards and villains.

The only creature in the house who could patrol rafters and vents without knocking over an entire display of holiday garlands.

She nudged the ornament again, this time more thoughtfully. It glimmered like moonlit ice.

"Do you think the same person left both gifts?" Clara asked, brow furrowing.

"Someone who knows the truth," Amelia said slowly. "Someone who wants it protected."

Lady Grey flicked an ear.

Someone who appreciated her work, clearly. Someone who understood that while humans argued and panicked and spilled far too much cocoa, *she* had been the one doing all the important running, leaping, and pawing at suspicious objects.

About time.

Amelia reached for the ornament. "Let's put this on the tree—"

Lady Grey swatted her hand away with a firm—yet polite—tap.

Amelia's brows rose, amused. "No?"

Lady Grey placed both paws over the ornament and dragged it toward her chest.

Clara snorted. "I think she wants to keep it."

Amelia's smile softened. "Then it's hers."

Yes.

It was hers.

She curled around the ornament, settling beside the fire where warmth seeped deliciously into her fur. Her tail draped across her nose; her paws tucked neatly beneath her chest. The silver cat nestled securely against her.

The inn felt warm again.

Calm again.

Safe again.

For now.

Amelia and Clara's voices drifted around her—talk of brunch, guests, and whether the roads would reopen by evening. Outside, the snow fell in lazy flakes instead of frantic sheets. Inside, the tree lights cast gentle halos across the room.

Lady Grey slipped in and out of drowsy contentment, her purr rumbling like a tiny engine of pride and peace.

This was Christmas.

She had done well.

Her inn was safe.

Her humans were safe.

Her ornament was safe.

She began to drift.

Then—

A sound.

Faint.

Familiar.

Impossible.

Lady Grey's ears twitched.

She lifted her head.

Clara's words faltered. Amelia froze mid-sentence.

"What was that?" Clara whispered.

The sound came again—threading up from the lower floor, curling through the quiet halls like a ghost left over from the storm.

A gentle chime.

A precise, tinkling melody.

Soft and haunting and unmistakable.

Covington's music box.

Playing.

By itself.

Amelia rose slowly to her feet, one hand pressed to her chest. "But... the sheriff took the evidence."

"All of it," Clara breathed. "Including the box."

Lady Grey stood in one fluid motion, silver ornament still hugged to her chest like a tiny, precious shield.

Her fur bristled.

Someone had returned.

Or something had been left behind.

The melody floated through the air again—clearer now, sweeter and eerier all at once.

Amelia whispered, "That's impossible."

Clara's eyes were wide. "We're not alone."

Lady Grey's tail puffed into a grey bottlebrush.

With a low, warning growl, she hopped down from her cozy spot by the fire. The ornament clinked softly against the floorboards as she padded to the top of the staircase.

She paused—ears high, whiskers forward—listening.

Down below, in the shadows of the old inn, the music box played its eerie tune.

Calling.

Waiting.

Lady Grey's eyes narrowed.

Christmas might not be quite finished after all.

Epilogue

The Spirit of the Inn

The inn came back to life one week after Christmas.

Not all at once—Tumblebrook never did anything all at once—but gradually, patiently, like a lantern flame coaxed back from the edge of a fading ember. First came the scent: cinnamon drifting from the kitchen as Clara experimented with a "peace pie" that, despite its optimistic name, involved a slightly alarming amount of nutmeg.

Then came the sounds: cheerful knocks on the front door, neighbors dropping off belated gifts, and the soft rumble of travelers returning to the North Shore after the storm.

Finally—hesitantly, then steadily—the laughter returned.

And the inn breathed again.

Amelia stood at the reception desk updating the winter reservations ledger, pausing every so often just to listen. Children raced down the hall toward the fireplace. Boots clomped over the entry rug. Someone in the parlor tuned a violin for the holiday encore show the town insisted on hosting.

The storm, the grief, the tension that had wrapped tightly around her heart for days—

—all of it had finally lifted.

She closed the ledger with a soft thump and inhaled the comforting blend of pine garlands and warm apple cider.

"That's the last of the records?" Clara asked as she arrived with a fresh plate of cranberry scones.

"Finally. Everyone's check-ins are sorted through January." Amelia stretched her fingers. "Next year, please remind me not to fill the inn to capacity during a winter festival."

Clara smirked. "And rob us of the chaos? Absolutely not."

Lady Grey—perched atop the counter like a reigning monarch—purred in agreement.

Amelia chuckled and scratched under the cat's chin. "Yes, yes. You survived another holiday circus. Barely."

Lady Grey flicked her tail, scandalized at the suggestion of struggle.

Clara crossed her arms. "Speaking of circus... have you heard from the museum?"

Amelia's eyes brightened. "The curator emailed?"

Clara grinned. "Everything's official. The Monarch relics are cataloged and will be transported to Duluth this weekend. They'll be part of the spring exhibit on North Shore history."

Warmth filled Amelia's chest—deep and glowing.

"So... they're going to tell the truth."

"All of it," Clara said. "No secrets. No cover-ups. Just history, finally set right."

Amelia glanced toward the parlor doorway. The Christmas tree—still proudly decorated—sparkled with new ornaments donated by guests. Near the center hung a small silver cat ornament, gleaming like a shard of starlight.

Lady Grey's ornament.

Her well-earned badge of victory.

"We made the right decision," Amelia murmured.

Clara nudged her. "You made the right decision."

"No," Amelia said softly. "We all did. Doris, Mr. Lark, Ezra...

even Sheriff Daniels. Tumblebrook came together, even after everything."

Clara's expression softened. "Forgiveness is our strongest tradition."

"And trust," Amelia echoed.

Lady Grey yawned—dramatically uninterested in sentimental human reflections—and hopped to the floor. Her tail swished regally as she trotted toward the window.

Clara leaned closer and whispered, "You know Daniels was right about one thing."

"Oh?"

"Lady Grey absolutely deserves the 'Detective of the Year' award."

Amelia laughed—a bright, genuine sound she hadn't felt in her chest in far too long. "Oh, don't tell her that. She already thinks she runs the place."

"She does run the place."

"I know."

Clara's hand rested briefly on Amelia's arm. "We're lucky," she said quietly.

"Why's that?"

Clara motioned toward the bustling inn—the guests, the snow, the soft music. "Because even when things fall apart—even when secrets crawl out of old shadows—we manage to come back together. Every time."

Amelia felt her heart swell. "Yes. We do."

A sharp cry interrupted them.

Lady Grey sat on the windowsill, pawing insistently at the glass, golden eyes locked on the front lawn.

"What now?" Clara murmured, stepping closer.

Amelia joined her.

Outside, fresh snow blanketed the world in soft white. The garden lamps glowed amber against the drifts. The great spruce tree —still trimmed in festival lights—stood proudly in its snowy circle.

Beneath it, a lone figure stood.

A woman in a long dark coat, scarf tucked neatly beneath her collar. Snowflakes clung to her hair, turning the dark strands to shimmering silver. She held something in her gloved hand.

A rose.

White.

Fresh.

Amelia's breath caught. "Oh."

Clara's voice softened. "Is that...?"

"Yes," Amelia whispered. "Covington's daughter."

She hadn't spoken at her father's service. Hadn't lingered afterward. Her grief had been quiet, distant—wrapped around her like an old winter shawl—but it had run deep. Deeper than words could carry.

Now she knelt beneath the spruce, placing the rose gently at its base. Snow swirled around her in delicate eddies.

Lady Grey quieted, sensing the gravity of the moment.

Amelia touched the windowpane. Cold seeped into her palm.

"She came to say goodbye," she murmured.

"Or to forgive him," Clara whispered.

The woman rose, brushed snow from her gloves, and looked toward the inn—not at Amelia, not at any single window, but at the place itself. A soft, knowing expression touched her features.

Then she turned and walked into the snowfall, leaving the rose behind.

Lady Grey pressed her forehead gently to the glass.

Amelia blinked back warm, stinging tears.

The inn glowed softly behind them. The town murmured with life. Outside, winter fell in peaceful silence, blanketing the world in something gentle.

"Think she'll come back someday?" Clara asked quietly.

"Yes," Amelia said after a long moment. "I think she will."

Lady Grey purred—low and approving.

Amelia smiled, wrapping her arms around herself. "Come on," she said. "Let's get ready for tonight. Guests will be hungry."

Clara grinned. "Then let's make it a feast."

They stepped back into the warmth, leaving the window behind.

But Lady Grey lingered a moment longer.

Watching.

Listening.

Guarding.

Because Tumblebrook wasn't quite done with mysteries.

Not yet.

But tonight—tonight, it breathed in peace.

And Lady Grey, Detective of the Year, was exactly where she belonged:

At home.

At the inn.

At Amelia's side.

Watching the snow fall.

The Night Before Christmas

'Twas the Night of the Mystery at Tumblebrook Inn (Serious)

Twas the night before Christmas in Tumblebrook town,
  Snow drifted like feathers on rooftops of brown.
  The garlands were hung by the bannister stair,
  In hopes that warm laughter soon would be there.
  Amelia bustled, the inn shining bright,
  While Lady Grey prowled through the soft candlelight.
  Clara baked cookies with spice in the air,
  Unaware of the secrets soon stirring with care.
  When out in the parlor there rose such a crash,
  They rushed from the kitchen in one sudden dash.
  There under the tree in a tangle of green
  Lay poor Mister Covington—no longer serene.
  He clutched a glass ornament shattered in two,
  While whispers of treachery chilled the whole crew.
  The storm sealed them in—no escape, no reply,
  Till morning could summon the sheriff nearby.

Clara found notes with cryptic commands,
"For those who seek truth..." written by shadowed hands.
Lady Grey, whiskers sharp, took to the floor,
Revealing, with paw swipes, each hidden clue more.
They searched every nook, every attic and hall,
Where footsteps and whispers crept soft by the wall.
The ornaments' secrets, once gilded with grace,
Led straight to a plot the town long tried to trace.
A spy in the rafters, a poisoner near,
A comeback of Monarch they all came to fear.
Doris and Lark in their grief intertwined,
Old wounds from the past they were forced to unwind.
Till Clara and Amelia chased through the snow,
And truth spilled like lanterns' warm holiday glow.
The villain was caught as the storm broke at last,
His Monarch-tied schemes now a tale of the past.
On Christmas morn, healing embraced every soul,
Forgiveness spread gently, making broken hearts whole.
And Lady Grey curled by the fire's soft gleam,
The true Christmas detective—queen of the scene.
But outside the inn, 'neath the evergreen tree,
A lone rose was placed with a quiet dignity.
Covington's daughter, in snowfall so light,
Paid respects to her father that still winter night.
And Amelia whispered as peace filled the air,
"Merry Christmas to all, and may truth ever fare."

'Twas the Night Before Chaos at Tumblebrook Inn (Parody)

'Twas the night before Christmas, when all through the inn,

Not a creature was stirring—except Clara in a spin.

The cookies were burning, the cider too hot,

And Lady Grey judged them from her favorite spot.

The garlands were crooked, the tree lights a mess,

But Amelia still smiled through the holiday stress.

For the festival crowds were arriving in packs—

Which of course meant chaos (and one or two snacks).

When out in the parlor arose such a clatter,

Clara dropped her whisk to see what was the matter.

And what to their wondering eyes should appear,

But Covington—dramatic—face-first in reindeer.

An ornament shattered lay crushed in his grip;

Lady Grey sniffed it and thought, *He tripped.*

But no—humans gasped, as humans will do,

And said, "Could it be... someone made him go blue?"

The storm sealed them in—oh, what perfect timing—

A murder! A blizzard! And suspicious light diming!

Alden Pike panicked, Doris Finch fussed,

While Lady Grey rolled her eyes. *In humans we trust.*

Clara found notes in odd places they'd drop,

Like "For those who seek secrets" (or better: "Please stop").

Ezra muttered legends of ornaments old,

While Mr. Lark whispered, "This story's too bold."

Lady Grey took charge—as she does every case—

By climbing the rafters with elegance and grace.

She knocked clues from cubbies, from vents, and from shelves,

And generally solved things while humans fooled themselves.

A spy was revealed! Monarch schemes came to light!

The suspect then ran like a cat in the night.

Amelia gave chase with great northern flair,
While Clara shouted warnings like, "Don't slip! Don't you dare!"
At last, the culprit confessed with deep sighs
(After Lady Grey clawed at him—right in the thighs).
Sheriff Daniels arrived with his beard full of snow,
Saying, "Miss Farnsworth, please... could you lay low?"
But Christmas returned in warm Tumblebrook style,
With brunch, cozy fires, and cheer all the while.
Doris made amends, Mr. Lark made tea,
And Ezra vowed never to hire for free.
Lady Grey stretched proudly by the Christmas tree glow,
Thinking, *I saved this town—again, don't you know.*
When out in the snow, under twinkling light beams,
A stranger laid a rose (quite dramatic, it seems).
Clara said softly, "Do mysteries ever cease?"
Amelia answered, "No. But we like when they're least."
And Lady Grey winked (yes, cats wink on occasion):
"Happy Christmas to all—now fetch me crustacean."